Jane Burdiak recently retired from teaching and continues to be inspired and uplifted by life going on around her.

Also by Jane Burdiak

Patchwork

Domestic Science

BETWEEN THE STARS

For
Robert

Jane Burdiak

Between The Stars

AUSTIN MACAULEY
PUBLISHERS LTD.

A CIP catalogue record for this title is available from the British Library.

ISBN 978 184963 375 8

www.austinmacauley.com

First Published (2013)
Austin Macauley Publishers Ltd.
25 Canada Square
Canary Wharf
London
E14 5LB

Printed and Bound in Great Britain

THE BEGINNING

She sat deep in her grandmother's Lord Loom chair watching her son pack. Like stepping stones neat piles of belongings were organised across the carpet, waiting to be plunged into the dark depths of the rucksack leaning against the bed. Apart from the odd word neither of them said anything. Once again it was time to leave, to say good-bye, to say take care, to say I love you.

There was an eerie powdery silence. As if the first day of term was not bad enough, her spirits dropped even further when she drew back the curtains. Silently, during the night, whispering flakes had gently fallen to form a drifting, rolling wilderness of pure snowdrop white. It was not a dream. Immediately she was tense and worried about driving. She was no radio ham but tuned in to a local station to listen for news on school closures. The grating high-pitched frequencies had to one of the worst sounds ever. Beneath the glass the red needle slowly made its way across the wavebands eventually making a controlled landing on Three Counties Radio, but it didn't tell her what she wanted to hear. There were no closures.

The term started and the first week ended. There were exam papers to mark and she spent the entire weekend doing so. The handwriting from some was illegible and the spelling was worse. She translated 'achitment' as equipment.

Sad news was vibrating and lighting up the bedside cupboard. Her husband's dear mother had died, finally giving up the battle of living. Even though she had not been able in the last few years, she had still been there, the linchpin, presiding over her family, there to be included and thought about. Understandably her husband felt an immense loss, his mind flooded with private memories. She had known her for over forty years and as she tried to sleep she remembered her, a hardworking, enduring woman who did not impose or intrude, but allowed her to be herself, without criticism. Her legacy would live on through the generations, though her children, her grandchildren, whom she adored and her great-grandchildren whom she showered with pure indulgent love. Without her, they could not be. She reached out and rested her hand on her husband's arm. She squeezed it gently.

When would the winter darkness end?

She had finished, or thought she had finished writing her second book. It had to end. But during the night and driving to school there was a void, a quiet emptiness. She was at a loss. Her active mind had become used to stringing together a necklace of words, of cultivating the bones of a paragraph or untangling a matted chapter in her fraying patchwork life. Picking up the pen again she opened her new notebook, a special notebook, given with love from her friend the previous summer and she began to write, not a book, just random thoughts. Not only did she write in her notebook, but on anything that came to hand, receipts, memos, car parking tickets that had accrued in the pocket of her car and on the back of shopping lists. Like a reporter she wrote at anytime, anywhere. Christmas and New Year had curtailed any activity at the publishers and maybe the current climate too, but nonetheless she bravely emailed. Was there a date? How was the progress? She waited. Then, in the inbox, there was a message. She had waited and waited for months and now that she knew, she was filled with a mixture of fear, dread and excitement. A few days later she checked her emails again. There on the screen was her door curtain, depicted as the cover of her book along with a brief outline of the story that had started in a stifling Spanish courtyard and ended in the back garden.

She lay in bed burning, every blood vessel reaching the surface of her skin. Sleep was impossible. Inside, her body was dancing, jiving and bopping, reeling with excitement. Deep in her pillow her heart pounded. Alert to every sound, her husband's breathing shuffled quietly beside her and on the table the clock yapped repeatedly like a small bored dog. Over and over in her head she was singing 'I did it, I did it'. Like Henry Higgins she too, had done it, proving that all things were possible. Fuzzy shades of grey loomed around the room.

All week, she had given up her precious time after school to help the pupils with their coursework.

After two weeks of penetrating cold, the sun came out and the wind blew the washing dry. She ventured to the end of the garden to admire the harbinger of spring, clusters of snowdrops, nestled under the apple tree. She shed her coat when she walked into town.

For the second week, she had given up her precious time after school to help the pupils with their coursework. Chris tended to do as little as possible during lessons, and at parents' evening on Thursday evening she planned to inform his parents and make them aware. She showed them two 'A' grade projects, both completed by boys a few years ago, then showed them their son's work. His parents leaned forward on the mean polyurethane chairs, anxious and not wanting to hear what she had to say, confronting their son with uncomfortable questions and an even more uncomfortable silence. A look of disappointment passed between them. Chris sat slumped, for once with nothing to say. He had let his parents down. He had let her down. He had let himself down. The next day he proudly showed her the work he had completed when he had got home and after school on Friday evening he stayed to do some more.

'All Things Bright and Beautiful'. She knew every verse and the chorus, learnt off by heart and remembered from the daily assemblies at junior school. Until she started singing she had been composed, but the words came out all wrong or not at all, her mouth left to shape the words in between gulps of air. Out in the low midday sun the mourners waited for the coffin to make the short journey to the cemetery. Around her everything carried on as normal, the postman on his bike in his bright orange jacket, the steady movement of traffic, a siren in the background. The pall bearers carefully balanced their feet on the wooden boards covered with synthetic grass, similar to that used in greengrocer's displays of lovingly arranged vegetables and lowered the coffin gently into the ground. The priest murmured softly. Long shadows stretched across the wet grass. Some stepped forward, bravely fighting back the tears, their hearts labouring and heavy with grief. Bare hands reached blindly into the box of earth, scattering their final farewell over their mother, their grandmother and their friend, too numb to say goodbye.

For the third week, she had given up her precious time after school to help the pupils with their coursework.

On Thursday the following week, there was good news. The first came at 6.30 a.m. when the phone rang. School was closed. During the night a crisp white tablecloth had been laid out across the land. Roads and paths merged under a thick blanket of white. Quilted gardens were fat with duvets of snow. Parked cars were cocooned and lampposts stippled. Gulls circled in the clear blue sky and swooped in the shivering cold, on the look out for food. Against the backdrop everything looked stark. Where people had moved about, the snow had compacted into a sheer, glassy surface. Just after nine she went out into the bright white light, wrapped against the stabbing cold and took herself into town. She had not gone far when a startling green and yellow City Link van hissed past in the slush, slowed down and cautiously pulled up in the lay-by opposite her house. She stopped in her tracks and waited, for what seemed like a long time. Then the van turned round, its tyres crunching the snow and parked outside her house. Gathering speed, she ran back, stepping high and leaping through the virgin snow, warm air escaped her mouth in little steamy puffs. The driver had a parcel under his arm and was walking towards the front door. She called as she neared the drive and he turned. Breathless she pushed the key into the lock then removing her gloves she hurriedly signed and printed her name on his list. Hastily saying goodbye she closed the front door, then kneeling down on the mat in the hall she excitedly opened the collapsing envelope secured with brown sticky tape.

Trembling, she held the book in her hands. Her book. Her name on the cover, her mother's name inside. Truly, it was a milestone, unbelievable, blurted out inside was a story, printed out, like a real book. Her story. Behind the cover of brightly coloured squares were her experiences and thoughts, an emotional journey, darned and stitched together to form a patchwork quilt of life. She was delirious.

All day she went around with a smile on her face. It had been a year since the sample chapter had been sent and two and a half years since she had taken the train to Brighton and the unfolding journey began, writing rapidly, almost incoherently on folded pieces of paper. Coming home, she remembered feeling embarrassed and secretive and at the time had not known that she was writing a novel, it was just her thoughts transferred from her mind and aired on paper. She had gone by herself and sat, not even thinking about her day on the pebbly beach, hiring a deck chair, the sun on her face and paddling in the cold English Channel. Nearer to home the train was practically empty. Feeling conspicuous, she felt that other people knew what she was doing. She had told no one. In fact it wasn't her intention to write a book at all. It just turned out that way. It was therapeutic and liberating and interesting and it amazed her that she could recall so vividly as though she had clicked on 'my memories' and there they were. It was important for her children to know how it was for their mother and their grandmother. It was a record, a document of quite ordinary activities and events that had shaped their lives and made them what they were. Like her old and shabby front door curtain, her book would be comfortable in the hand, supple and fading its spine would stand apart from all others on the shelf. With that, she went into the dining room and placed a copy of her book on the bookshelf between *The Book Thief* and *Nigella Express*. In bookshops, it would sit amongst the Bs leaning between John Bunyan and Anthony Burgess.

Returning to Brighton more recently, the day had left her feeling bereft, she had wanted to taste salt on her lips and wince later when she tried to brush the tangles from her hair, to sit against a wall out of the wind gulping big breaths of squally sea air, trying to read, but distracted too easily, a gull calling for her attention, or a boat prompting a bigger swell, disturbing her concentration when it broke on the shingle changing the regular wash and drag of the undertow pulling at the pebbles on the steep stony shelf; lifting her eyes from the fluttering pages of her book propped against her knees and to walk briskly along the front, leaning against the pressing wind, her clothes clinging to her shape, taking in familiar sights. But instead of feasting on the elements, it was glorious. For an hour she walked, like others, taking some exercise, breathing deeply, tasting as she passed the fish stalls en route, the softness of crab and the mean salty combination of anchovies wrapped around stuffed olives and threaded on sticks, both delights served in little polystyrene cups. The tantalizing sea sparkled and glittered. Outcrops of deckchairs were set out in twos for the endless flow of day-trippers and she indulged in a pink stripy one, removing it from its position and set it down nearer the sea, turning it to face the sun. It was a colourful scene. High in the clear blue sky above the wisps of cloud, planes crossed to Europe and against the arc of the horizon mariners sailed and chugged and drifted in the Channel, nearer, boats left a gleaming wake of steel and yellow buoys bobbed on the placid silvery surface, people swam and played where the water lapped and fizzled on the pebbles. All around there was murmuring, laughing and shrieks and the crunching of stones as people tried to walk. In order to grab all the day's attention she had gone on a commuter train, gliding into the swishy St Pancras International, then on to Farringdon and Blackfriars, where the train practically emptied, then to weave carefully through the capital and back into suburbia and beyond, where dazzling sunlight sprinkled like stardust through the trees that fringed the track, peppering the carriage with dark corners and spotted leopard light, when a man from nowhere handed her his camera and asked her to take his photo. Taking it seemed impossible, his black skin merged with the darkness and refused to be seen. He moved and sat nearer. She took it again and he looked at it. It wasn't how he wanted it to be. She took another and he smiled and thanked her when he saw it. The stations slipped past. With the prospect of a glimpse of the shimmering sea imminent, like a giddy child she became restless and began to get excited. Never tiring of the view, she had been many times, with her husband, with her children and on her own, going for no other reason than to be by the sea.

Always claiming that *Patchwork* had been her first fling with writing and in fact she was not one to write anything unless coerced, she was surprised to find when rummaging in a drawer, a worn piece of lined paper torn from an exercise book hand written in blue fountain pen. She would have been twelve or thirteen when she wrote 'My Sister' and it had been entered in the *Daily Telegraph* 'Young Writers Competition' in the early sixties, when their offices were in St Brides Street. Reading it through again, she felt that it had no merits. She had grown up in her shadow and it was nothing more than a jealous rebuke. Her friend thought otherwise.

Profile of a Living Person

My sister, bow-legged from riding Domino fancies herself as a model. Whether it be fashion or photographic, she stands for hours in front of a mirror wishing her legs to be a more pleasing shape. Heavy hipped and thick-thighed she will, night after night pinch and slap the fat into thin air until it throbbed then return to the mirror, standing in this pose and in that pose, picking a spot and painting a spot below her left eye, a natural mark of beauty.

Nothing is more important than her face. This she believes is her asset, but only when fabricated with various colours and textures then framed with a different head of hair pulled over her shabby worn out pan scourer. The finishing touches, a knotted neckerchief and turned-up coat collar to camouflage the craning throttle. Her name, she does have one is Fiona May.

My sister is a madam and always has been, she has had everything, whether begged, borrowed, bartered or bestowed. Fiona May could if she wanted to go out with any male, her choice of course. I wonder. She has such charm, such seductive persuasion with her boyfriends, they just cannot see anything wrong with her. Fiona is faultless. Often incredibly sweet and irresistibly feminine, well after admiring the mirror for two hours whatever else can they think? But oh! How blind.

She is the most ill-mannered, inconsiderate idler that was ever invented. A typical Sunday is spent rising at 1p.m., taking a mug of instant coffee, the medicine; a cigarette, the drug, gradually gaining strength then retiring again until 3 p.m. when she will go through the ritual of cleansing and healing the pimples and dark rings, replicas of the Saturday night and Sunday morning.

Fiona May has no qualms, she does not think that someone might disapprove of her conduct. Why should she care? In fact she would go out of her way to annoy or irritate, particularly while she was at school, an all-girls school where she was claimed to be eccentric for having green tinted glasses prescribed by the optician. She would have great delight in taking form captains position three times. How distasteful, thought her teachers. A typical Leo.

She is a leader in many ways, keen to invent something new and alive but is often inclined to slacken at the last minute. Fiona does not use her knowledge and abilities to their full extent, but then, why should she. An aggressive temperament creeps in, garnished with foul language and rudeness if the slightest words of advice are uttered. So where does one start … maybe at childhood? I wonder if she is my sister sometimes. Like the mirror, her boyfriends only see the surface.

I really do admire her though. She will accomplish everything she sets out to do, she has tremendous character, a great personality and guts. Fiona is my sister.

The sad bereavement, the furore of publication and the

adverse weather had each in their way hindered and distracted her from her thoughts, contributing to her lack of concentration. At school, work avoidance was punishable.

On Saturday morning, the first morning of the half term holidays she decided to go through the research and documents accumulated in her quest to put a name to the face of the boy in a photograph, found amongst her father's papers. Her search to find out who he was three years ago had led to the discovery of two separate families that she didn't know she had, but not the boy in the photograph. Finding Walter and finding Donald came as a complete surprise, even more so to them as they had not been looking. By now, the boy in the photograph would be in his sixties. There were no clues, no names, nothing to point her in the right direction. All three families plus the boy in the photograph were inextricably linked by one man, her father. Had she missed something? It was extremely difficult to place her father's whereabouts just after the war. All the evidence had been carefully placed in the lid of an A4 box, the photographs fastened together with arty plastic paper clips bought at the Museum of Modern Art in New York. Everything she had was there, but she couldn't work it out.

She pulled up the blind in the kitchen. The snowman, that had stood so proudly for over a week had lost his head. His green hat lay sodden in a puddle of Siberian water, his mouth had slipped down his body and the plums, used as eyes had been eaten by the blackbirds. The white wasteland was slowly dissolving. At last winter was relaxing. It was getting warmer.

Before returning to London in January, her son had joined her onto Genes Reunited. Familiarizing herself again with its various functions she sent some messages. She was not interested in family trees but found the 'trying to find' message boards extremely useful. She also explored the areas where her father's wartime mail had been re-directed.

Opposite arms, opposite legs, that was how she felt, pulled in all directions, reach, push, reach, stretch, arms out, travel. Her husband, her friends, her children, her schoolwork, her housework, her guilt and promoting her book were all grabbing her attention. Her week, her precious week had gone in a whirl. Not for a moment had she been at a loss.

On Monday she had retraced her steps and gone back with her friend to the villages nestled in the Warwickshire countryside, hoping to glean some information of her father's whereabouts during the war. They visited the cottages on the Banbury Road, discovered on a re-addressed envelope in 1945. Trying to find a Freda Evans who worked at Piper's Hill, they found Monica instead, who unfortunately was out. She left a scribbled note and her phone number, hoping that she would get back to her. It transpired that she was nothing to do with Freda.

On Wednesday, a lift in the car with her son to London, enabled an early start. He dropped her off in Cromwell Road at 8.45 a.m. and she took the District Line to Kew to do some research at The National Archive Office. Like others, she was early and sat in the foyer having a coffee to wait for the Reading Room to open at ten o'clock. Many sat with their laptops open or their phones pressed urgently to their ears, not able to relax and contemplate the need to be at the office in the first place. Apart from islands of mute computers waiting to tell and divulge secrets, hidden for years on dusty shelves, nothing interrupted the sterile view across the big airy room. A beige carpeted wasteland silenced quickening steps, anxious to sit down at a machine and log-on to their own private world. At the click of the mouse people leaned in, wanting to know, wanting to find out about, reading and scanning the screens, jotting things down. There was a quiet purposeful murmuring. She had gone to find out about twin boys, born in Birmingham in 1935. Her brother had sent a picture of his mother holding their hands. It was summer. It almost surprised her that she found the entry and read it several times before writing it down. The other thing that she had gone to find out was if her brother's mother was married to her father. She had told her son that she was. She scrolled through years of marriages before giving up and calling it a day.

Retired and older then her, the ladies faced her around the table. Wisps of white and greying hair framed their softness, their eyes bright and memories razor sharp, their zesty voices enthusiastic. She noticed that most wore glasses or had them ready, loosely cradled in their hands, or hanging from a chain around their necks or resting on the table beside them. They shared a common interest and met fortnightly to discuss the current book that they were all reading. They were finding the language in the present one hard going and needed a dictionary handy. Some words were not even in the dictionary. She was in the meeting room giving an informal talk to the reading group about her book, briefly outlining how it had come about and how it had come to be published. They were interested in what she had to say and knew each had a pressing story of their own to tell, they just hadn't put pen to paper, yet.

Another feature on Genes Reunited, not there before, was the facility to place a photo and this she tried without much success. Her three photos were grainy and old, the quality poor. Also, they were very small. She scanned them in. Oh, they looked awful, the image of the boy's face on one was totally obliterated. The photo that she named boy/girl was because she could not decide which he or she was. Hoping for breakfast, her son called after walking his dog. Well one good turn deserved another and she enlisted him to have a look at her abysmal efforts at scanning. He experimented with colour and mono-chrome and although the photos were black and white, colour looked surprisingly good. By showing the photos on Genes Reunited, it was her intention to jog a memory and throw some light. Without a name it was difficult. Maybe someone had the very same photos as her. Maybe they recognised the photo of her father as their father. She was hopeful and always optimistic. From her own experience she was sure that children would have a gut feeling about their parents. Surely the boy in the photo must have wondered, or questioned as he got older who his 'real' father was. Her father's insatiable salacious appetite to flirt was obvious to her, remembering his lecherous hands and his mouth searching for lips. Of course the photos could be completely innocent and if they were, it would put her mind at rest but she could not imagine her father treasuring pictures of his brothers' children, or anyone else's. People, especially people like her father simply did not do that. The picture of the boy had been looked at more often, exposure to the light had dulled the finish and it was creased and the corner was missing. She could not let sleeping dogs lie. From her various starting points she was determined to find out how it was.

On the 'trying to find' board, she left a message for the grandchildren of Annie and William, of which she was one. Carol replied, suggesting Scotland's People. Navigating the site was exacting. First she checked her grandparent's marriage, then looked on the birth register for their children. From previous information on her father's army records she pinpointed her uncles and there, listed on the screen, listed alphabetically were her father and his six brothers and all their children, well, nearly all, which until recently she had not known about. Now she needed to find out what cousins belonged to what uncle. She was particularly interested in finding the children belonging to Uncle Sam as she had discovered his name in one of her father's notebooks and finding him, she looked up his marriage, then the unusual second name and the corresponding date of birth of his daughter. It was slow going. The families were intertwined and because of the unusually large gap between Agnes born in 1920 and her sister in 1953 her father was still fathering children when his own children were. The first family of eight children lived in Scotland and when she met them for the first time they seemed to her like ageing aunts and uncles. The second family lived in Australia where a son grew up oblivious to his father and the third family was what she knew. It was while she was painstakingly trying to find out who the boy in the photograph was that she had come across the two families. Until then she didn't know that there was anything to find out, so had never thought to look.

The evening of her book launch at the library was upon her and she hoped for a good crowd. Chairs had been arranged neatly in rows staring blankly at the table, which apart from her book displayed on a perspex stand was completely empty. She positioned copies of her book ready for signing and fanned out the bookmarks on the table. A friend had brought along the most amazing cake and a bright red cyclamen gave the finishing touches. Just after six people began drifting in. More chairs were fetched, until there were no more and people stood. She talked for a few minutes then Ian read the piece about fire from the book. While he was reading, she had time to look around; there were so many people, friends she hadn't seen for ages, Brenda from the florists, Graham from the travel agents, friends and colleagues from school, Evelyn, her neighbour and her husband and children. She could hear them listening, then it was time for the all-important book signing. Many had come with several copies to sign, hoisting them out of cavernous bags and piling them on the table in front of her. Would she make mistakes? Would she spell her name wrong? Would she remember names? How much did they want her to write? She even had to write 'with love'. She was sparing with words like that and only written for special friends and those she really loved. Not even the library's copy was spared, everything was sold and she took that to mean that it had been a success. God she could do with a drink. But no, there was a school inspection happening in the morning and an early night was essential.

Weeks ago she had sent a copy of her book to Waterstone's head office for the fiction buyer to peruse, then on Saturday morning an envelope with a big 'W' on the postmark heralded the next step. The letter said that while they did not want to place a central order, Waterstone's stores were welcome to stock the book if they wished to and enclosed a store directory. Immediately she contacted her local branch to organize a book signing, then as so much of *Patchwork* had been set in Stirlingshire, she wrote to the store in Stirling, enclosing some promotional material. Perhaps they would they be interested in a book signing?

She left a message on the People's War website enquiring

about an extract on Piper's Hill. Within an hour an automated transcript had been returned. It wasn't useful.

Her friend, reading her book for the second time had drawn her attention to Helen and wanted to know more about her. She didn't know anything other than she had been a lodger and she remembered her clothes, her duster coats and stiletto heels and her hair worn in a bouffant. Who was Helen and why did she stay at their house? And why did she leave? Coming from Jedburgh, she assumed her to be Scottish, but checking on Scotland's People, found that was not the case. Helen had a sister called Pat, the same age as her. They had gone to the same school. She contacted Pat through Friends Reunited to find out about Helen. Most days she checked to see if she had replied. A week later, there had been no replies and she sent the message again.

The bright billowy weather gave way to days of grey oppressive skies, still and heavy with drizzle. When the cloud could hold on no longer, spots of rain darkened the pavement. Umbrellas ready.

Trying to find out about the past was frustrating. Every few days she checked to see if any of the contacts had got back to her. All her efforts were leading nowhere.

She wanted to know what people thought of her writing and what she had to say. Some read in disbelief. "Did Connie really eat dog food sandwiches?" Some found it harrowing and unsettling. Asked if she had found writing the book cathartic, she replied that maybe there was a sense of relief but what it had done was to open up a whole new world and she was standing on the edge. She was pleased to hear that they were moved by what she had written. Like a piece of fine art she had hoped for impact and wanted the reader to sit up and take notice. She hoped to leave the reader with a snapshot, to make them aware. Some people have no idea about other people's lives, unable to imagine the daily burden of prolonged abuse and its sustained draining of resources. She had written and drawn from her own experiences. Reading allowed a private access into other people's minds. Once, in *Oxford Modern* she had seen chilling images of an artist's work, haunting photographs of a deserted table and the debris of a half-eaten meal. The artist had brought to her attention the plight of ordinary people in the Middle East, their lives ripped apart and turned upside down, fleeing from everything they knew, to worse, to despair. The pictures were disturbing and still she thought of them. They made her feel helpless. The artist hadn't made it up or glamorised it, his camera showed it as it was and that was how she wanted her story to be. How it was. The book, like an old friend came into conversation with random people in the street or while stuffing the groceries into a bag at the check-out.

It was 2 a.m. and she was awake, wide-awake. She had a thought. She would have a party for her husband's birthday in June. It would be in the garden. It would be sunny. Now how would she arrange the tables? Snowy tablecloths would blow. Bunting would zigzag across the garden fluttering gently. There would have to be a set time for eating. There would be avocados and prawns and homemade hummus. It would be a surprise. Over and over the idea churned in her mind until eventually, she fell asleep.

Immediately, extensive lists were drawn up. Lists of people, lists of food, lists of drinks and a list of all the things that didn't fit into those categories. She was so excited. It was like Christmas in June. Quickly she made a triangular template from a cereal box. Old sheets, pillowslips, aprons and curtains were cut up to make the bunting and as soon as a decent length was machined together, and however late in the evening it was when she finished each section, she was out in the garden draping it from tree to tree. How it fluttered.

Her husband assumed that her sudden activity in rearranging furniture and painting the porch and removing weeds as soon as they appeared was for her brother's benefit.

She enlisted her husband, to fix the dripping bathroom tap and replace the non-existent grout, to construct a window box in front of the garage window and adjust the back door ever so slightly so that it didn't stick on closing. Her brother was due to arrive on the same day as the party. That was good and bad. The outside toilet was blitzed and she found herself selecting pot puree and air fresheners. Never in her life had she even thought of them, let alone bought them. She had a real aversion to their obnoxious smells. Did people really waste their money on such frivol? The choice was extensive but in the end it was more the colour than the smell that decided what she chose, shades of white and cream for the bathroom and earthy browns for the outside toilet. The gelatinous tongues of air fresheners were obscured from view, placed discreetly out of sight. Not keen on the hook over the bowl style, lemon scented foaming tablets were dropped into the cisterns. She bought a set of little hand towels and folded them neatly in a basket on the corner of the bath, she bought a box of tissues, another luxury, and pulled one out to look as though it was something that she always had. She washed a dusty basket of shells and left them on the sill as a feature. She did not want to be remembered for her poor latrine arrangements. Not usually galvanized into domestic action, she quietly enjoyed the transformations.

Apart from the fraying on some and complete absence of fabric on others due to too much sitting doing homework and revising, the flattened foam and greasy marks from a thousand meals, she was entirely happy with her dining room chairs but couldn't have the visitors seeing such a state of disrepair. They were long overdue for a make-over and although it was not beyond her capabilities she preferred to have them repaired professionally and leaned into the book case for the big fat Yellow Pages. There were not many upholsterers listed. She phoned the nearest one, not wanting to spend time travelling around. A time was arranged to deliver the 'drop-ins' as they were called along with the fabric she had chosen. The premises were completely shuttered except for where the door used to be. That too was shuttered but partly open for her benefit. She tapped and ducked underneath. She stood in the cool dusty darkness. Adjusting to the light she was surrounded by an accumulated tangle of miscellaneous possessions stacked to the ceiling and reaching the walls. In the restricted space she could see planks of wood, old beds, shelves, boxes, old tools etc. Everything seemed to be covered in a layer of cement coloured dust. A lawn mower prevented her from going further and in the distance, beyond the gloomy room full of shabby dingy chaos in which she was wedged, she could see the workroom bathed in a magical golden shaft. Like a spotlight the sun fell on the most beautiful armchair being upholstered in straw coloured damask. She could hear a radio. She called hello. She called again. A wiry little man, seeming older than her, appeared and picked his way through the minefield. She balanced the bag of 'drop-ins' on the nearby garden fountain and not wanting to mark it, she showed him the fabric in mid-air, deciding which side would be the right side, even though either would have done. He said that he would call in a week's time and to mind her head as she left. She ducked under the shutter again into the blinding bright sunshine. Returning a week later, the armchair had gone. Once home, she pressed the 'drop-ins' snugly into the gaping mouths beneath the table.

Getting ready for the influx of sixty friends without her husband's knowledge, was no mean feat. Everything had to be done when he was out of the house. Invitations were sent out and replies sent to school or via email. Glasses and wine were stored under beds and in the airing cupboard. Sets and sets of plates along with cutlery and serving dishes were bought from charity shops, put through the dishwasher then hidden. She bought a fridge and borrowed another. Although much of the food was prepared and frozen in advance, a lot had to be dealt with on the day. No expense was spared. Creating it was such a pleasure and gave her such a buzz. There was no way she would have bought anything already prepared. Some shops sold platters of nibbles, they looked nice enough but tasted of nothing. She wanted her guests to experience subtle flavours, to remember how food should taste, to be able to return to the table for more.

Sunday 14th June 2009. And so it was, that the party that had kept her awake back in April, happened.

At this stage, still having no idea of the party ahead, her husband set off for Heathrow airport. By 3.45 a.m. the garden was a hive of activity. The table, 32ft long was built and laid with snowy white tablecloths, the bunting was strung up and the balloons blown up. Geraniums lined the entrance at the back gate. A barrel of lager was installed before 7 a.m. and the contents well and truly tested by 7.30 a.m. Her son, an expert in the field, positioned coloured lamps ready for the evening and a sophisticated sound system. A web of lights was thrown over the great conifer hedge. Nearer the house, tables were laid for the food. A great stack of plates, all the cutlery that she possessed and all the freshly ironed napkins were placed at one end in the shade of the pergola along with the glasses, all shapes and sizes. A glorious still calm day dawned. The ordered wall-to-wall sky of blue was suspended.

It was getting nearer and nearer to meeting her brother. Almost sixty years since he left with his mother, he returned. The man from Australia arrived at quarter to eight in the morning. Along with the savoury smells his presence filled the kitchen. His strong stance was striking, very upright, large scale and long limbed, but not willowy, but not cushions of fat either even though the buttons on his denim shirt stretched to bursting around his ample paunch. His mass of grey hair with flashes of white was unruly and wild. He wore large framed varifocal tinted glasses. He showed no sign of uncertainty. He moved round the table to where she was standing up to her elbows in flour, and gave her a big sisterly hug. Moving back, struck dumb; head shaking followed and they looked at each other unable to say anything. The plan had originally been to have a traditional breakfast but the pressure to get on with party preparations was suddenly the priority, suggesting a cup of tea instead followed by a few hours' sleep.

In the kitchen, there was too much to do. It was intense. Looking at the clock and the one o'clock deadline she had set herself, there were moments when she ground to a complete stop. No wonder people bought the readymade platters. Breathing deeply, she pressed on. More oven space would have been good. Her children were priceless. They kept her going when she thought she could manage no more. There was food everywhere. Putting the finishing touches to desserts was so exacting, placing raspberries and piping cream, removing cheesecakes from tightly fitting containers, no space to put them, her heart pounding, her fingers fumbling. People began to arrive. She ran in and out to meet and greet. Her husband was effervescent, totally overwhelmed. She could hear his voice from the kitchen, lifted and energized, meeting friends not seen for years. Laughing. It was good to hear him laugh. Like a galleon in full sail the table ripped across the garden. The bunting fluttered from mast to mast. Everyone was on deck, talking and laughing, eating and recording the scene.

She had made her April dreams come true. Only when the last of the desserts had been finished did she start to relax. The afternoon drifted into the evening, when all but a few friends had said their goodbyes. As daylight withdrew the lights came into their own, claiming the garden, transforming it into a film set. The hedge was festooned with twinkling stars. It was magical, an enchanted mysterious world of isolated arbours buried deep in the jungle. Pools of light lured the eye into purple caverns and grottos, thick with eerie hanging plants that lurked and beckoned. Lit up, shrubs and plants looked extreme, leaping from the earth like pyrotechnics or cowering bulky shadows that at any time would unfold and bare their gnashing teeth. Secret paths disappeared into a maze of inky coverts.

His brogue was strange and foreign and she quickly learned another language, cow was milk, wing was arm, chuck was egg, road kill was an animal lying dead in the road and maybe put in a pie, hosing down was heavy rain and the 'ute' was her brother's utility vehicle used for driving short distances. Having sent photos she was thankful that he did not look like her father, their father. But not until he had been with her some time did she begin to notice similarities. His feet, that were bare most of the time and wedged into rubber flip-flops were like his. For a man of his height, his feet were small, the arches high, the texture and pink colour of the skin was the same. She remembered seeing her mother on her hands and knees trying to ease socks over her father's stubborn inflexible blocks of wood, stretching the cuff to its limit to avoid scuffing the creepy skin and his lashing tongue. Like her father, the palms of his hands roamed over his big hard stomach, impregnated with years of indulgence and over-eating, sometimes resting them, fingers interlocked on the brow. In frustration one day, he shook a piece of paper at her, torn from the *Daily Mail* that she hadn't dealt with, demanding that she got on with it. She had heard that tone before, a long time ago when she was a child. At the Festival of Speed he picked up a pair of sunglasses off the dry trampled grass and handed them to her as though he was giving her something, her father, their father would have done that. She still had books on the bookshelf that he had 'acquired' and given to her as presents. Like the sunglasses they meant nothing. Another time, she was wrestling with a roll of bin bag liners. His eyes were on her as she teased, or unsuccessfully tried to tease the bag open. It didn't go without comment, implying stupidity. Inadvertently she had been trying to open the sealed end. She just laughed. "I haven't got my glasses on." Disappointingly he was like his father and she knew that whenever she tore off a bin bag liner, she would revisit the scene in the kitchen. Her lack of interest in modern technology bothered him, no mobile, no microwave, no 'sat-nav', nothing more than basic understanding of computers. No desire to read the paper. There were habits, minor irritations really that she found annoying, his vice like hands annihilating a beer can beyond recognition or his flip flops flipping and flopping, or his perpetual long drawn out sighs.

The arrival of her brother heralded the approaching storm. In the early days when the weather was good he sat outside along with her husband where the space was big, where the garden took care of their voices. They immersed themselves in reading. Her brother spread the newspaper on the table, his forearms checking the pages if the wind ruffled them. He read it all and it took all day. Her husband continued reading a book, started weeks ago, with over a thousand pages of print, a doorstop so heavy that it needed a lectern to hold it. In between snatches of reading they spent their time talking and drinking cups of tea before twelve and glasses of beer after. Now and then her husband would attend to the garden, watering pots, or transplanting a tray of lettuces, or trimming the hedge. Being tolerant and understanding was not one of his strengths and she was pleased and proud of the way he had adjusted to this complete stranger. He was pleasant and sociable. One warm day merged with another. The day extended into the evening when the shade crept across the grass and still they sat in the vanishing light, along with her and anyone else who just happened to drop in for dinner, until something good on television dragged them indoors or an unwelcomed chill sent them in search of something warm to wear.

But the weather changed and so did her husband. The tectonic plates were shifting. His face went behind a cloud, his jaw set firm, his eyes distant. Determined crow's feet etched deeply between his eyebrows and if he spoke which occasionally he did through gritted teeth, his voice was monotonous, barely audible and lacked sincerity. Tuneless lack-lustre whistling, amounting to three bland notes in the key of D accompanied his apathy and warned of his impending presence. Vacant eyes looked but didn't see. With his morbid fascination of the war and loathing of the Russians, he buried his head deeper into his bible of a book. Feeling orphaned she searched his soul, hoping to find a reason for his indifference towards her but his tawny eyes, loaded with contempt had lost their warmth shutting her out. After a while she stopped searching. She guessed that he felt marginalized, elbowed out, because another man had encroached upon his territory, taking advantage of the spoils, muscling in, the centre of attention, dominating, antagonizing, goading him, stretching his legs under the table, sitting in his place at the kitchen table, the favourite table, the favourite place. Her husband did not like sharing her with anybody. He felt threatened. He had no need. Conversation was polite. "Do you have fog?" she asked her brother. Her husband should have known better, but his clouded judgement was blurred. On seeing the French stick, still warm from the Co-op, her husband asked if he could have some filled with cheese and tomato. She cut off a quarter of the loaf and filled it as requested. For lunch an hour later he asked for the same again and a piece to take fishing. She made the last quarter for her brother and took it, along with a coffee to where he was sitting. She went without. It didn't occur to her husband that she had had nothing. He didn't see why other people in the house should have her care and undivided attention.

Without complaining she had given everything to the success of her brother's visit and was quite prepared to be the perfect hostess. Cooking, shopping, washing, ironing, housework, completed with minimum fuss and maximum streamlined efficiency along with endless hours spent talking. There was no let up.

Besides cooking in the height of summer and tension in the air the intense heat came on suddenly, sweat sprung from her body without warning. Underneath the skin, burned like a furnace, out of control, radiating from the epicentre of her body, each wave heightening and increasing in strength until the built-up pressure was so great that it forced its way through the fissures of tissue and muscle, through organs and entwining sinews to burst through the epidermis. With the onset of delirium she was suicidal and when she could no longer stand it she would throw off the covers, fling wide the window or strip off the cardigan to hold it inside out while the fire consumed. Relief from the heat followed just as suddenly, as a layer of tingling pin-pricking sweat permeated out of every pore, as though an army of ants had bitten all at the same time, leaving in its wake a moist glistening film clinging to her face. Her complexion was a florid, blotchy bloom as though she had been standing over a copper for hours puddling the laundry and a clammy thundery feeling left her feeling weak. Even her scalp smelled like a dog left out in the rain. Her damp hair pasted itself to the nape of her neck. Where her clothes had touched her skin they were wet, she knew that later the folds would dry into salty vapour trails and until the spasm passed, it was hard to concentrate on anything.

Her husband's behaviour wounded and betrayed. She felt dislocated, lost and miserable. She called him while she was away, to say that she had arrived, she called again to update him on her progress. He was hostile. From his tone, she wondered if he had noticed that she had gone. He was apathetic and not interested in what she had to say. He didn't hear. He wasn't listening. There was no affection, no love in his voice. She didn't phone again. Arriving home, he didn't say hello and ask her how she was but wished instead that she had been away for at least another month. Feeling alienated and totally abandoned she was left to cope with broken doors swinging precariously on rusty hinges and shattered panes that let in a whistling tormenting wind along with the ghosts, ghosts that crept about her mind, scaring and haunting her imagination.

Like a fugitive, she sought the sanctuary of her car. Sinking heavily into its dopey warmth, protected by its thin blue metallic shell she escaped the taunting atmosphere thick with jealousy and resentment that had accumulated, silently pinning her against the wall, stifling her very existence. Sometimes she left the house earlier than necessary and sat folded in thought, where no one could see the sadness in her eyes or hear her wavering voice. It was her safe haven. Usually she loved the tranquillity, the solitude of early mornings especially, busying herself uninterrupted, no one to disturb and distract her from her thoughts, life springing from the tap, the low cluck of the fridge and the kettle boiling for company, its florescent light clicking off, familiar sounds, loyal and dependable, inanimate objects that asked nothing of her. She loved too, the easy going companionable silence when bouts of stillness fell upon a conversation, allowing time to reflect, allowing time to think and take things in but the loud oppressive silence surrounding her was unbearable.

Entranced, she lay listening to the everlasting night breathing, to the tall black poplars across the road, the swell of their branches like a heaving sea. They dwarfed the pollarded willows. Planted as saplings at least twenty years ago the poplars had quietly grown, the gentle muttering leaves long gone. Their whispering had become a swaying darkness, shushing like the receding tide relentlessly dragging pebbles back below the surface, leaving a fringe of foam. Being awake during the night used to bother her, but over time she had become used to it even looked forward to the nightly episodes of dreams and reality merging, a video of scenes playing through her mind, maybe stopping to pause or rewind or fast forward. She used the quiet of night to write in her mind. Through the gap in the curtains the light from the streetlights fell across the bed and slashed the wardrobe door in half. Occasionally when a car passed, its beam cast an arc of whispering shadows that quietly scrolled across the ceiling. She was accustomed to the dim colourless room, the looming grey shapes. Through closed eyes she estimated the time. Gradually the darkness thinned to a murky dawn and their colour returned.

She too lost herself in books. They nourished her mind and distracted from the awfulness of it all. An extension to her arm, they went everywhere with her. When she was not reading, when she was peeling potatoes or stirring a sauce they were close by, closed with a bookmark indicating where to open it again or placed open, face down on the dresser or a chair waiting to be picked up when the reading resumed. Reading soothed, and she would doze on her faded blue deck chair, her fingers holding the fluttering pages open. When there was conversation, she commented on what was happening in the story or the characters or the places in the book. Reading transported her back in time and across seas. Her preferred genre was a blend of fact with fiction but whatever book she read, she was in it, there with the characters, enduring whatever was dealt. Drawn to the horror of war her books took her to occupied France, the Crimea and Afghanistan. In the safety of her Englishwoman's castle she saw herself as the victim, stones forced into her mouth, her teeth chipped and broken or freezing to death while on guard duty. She could imagine how it was for the children in the foreign fields of *Five Quarters of the Orange*. Years ago, while holidaying she had walked in the shimmering afternoon, with her husband and children to the quiet cool waters of the Loire. The punishing heat closed in. It was hushed and airless. The dizzy fizz of insects sedated and the birds silenced in the pressing sun. Little clouds of dust kicked up as their bare sandaled feet pressed into the dry dusty track between the ripening harvest and scattered poppies. She could imagine how it felt for Sam, returning from Burma, shell shocked, yet surviving all, but wanting more, more than the predictable grey wet slates of Cumbria or William trying to black out the horror of war, seeking refuge in the labyrinth of sewers beneath Victorian London. She suffered hardship and deprivation in the damp rat infested tenements in London's East End. Living in squalor she had nothing. Reading made her own situation pale into insignificance, it was nothing in comparison to the fear and despair experienced by the characters and how they showed courage and resilience in rebuilding their fragile fragmented lives. She read books to the bitter end. Re-reading the thin yellowing pages of the *Thorn Birds*, she found the type set too close and missing its front cover it was awkward to hold comfortably. No longer, her cup of tea, she was impatient to finish it, but finish it she did.

House arrest was how it felt. Crushed and held in custody in her own home, the immediate vicinity her exercise yard, where she would put out the bins on Monday mornings, hang out the washing, fold the washing, cut the grass, clean the windows. She would walk or cycle into town for things that she had run out of, carrying milk and bread precariously on her handlebars, the handles of the bag stretched to their limit or if walking, swapping the weight from one hand to the other. No one offered to get the milk. Her self-imposed boundary was set in her mind. She wondered that if she did venture beyond the barbed wire fence on the edge of town, she would ever come back and was tempted when occasionally on parole to take her passport and necessary documents in case she didn't. She could not allow herself her freedom. When she met friends, she could not be her true self. She could not look friends in the eye and be honest. They would have recognized her torment and she would have crumbled into a blubbering heap. "I can't talk about it now." She would say. It almost seemed safer to remain confined to barracks, imprisoned in self-pity. She could see no way out. The situation had to be endured. She couldn't do what she wanted to do when she wanted to do it, having to use the computer in the early morning when her brother who was always logged on, was asleep. She couldn't fall asleep in the garden without being disturbed. She couldn't whip cream or make a cake or chug around with the vacuum cleaner, or dry her hair without complaint. When the washing machine was spinning at a thousand revs per minute to bobble out of its position beneath the work top and stand in the middle of the kitchen floor still anchored to earth by its hoses, doors closed around the house. "When is that thing going to be finished?" Her husband blamed her for the leaky tap in the kitchen, saying that she turned it too tight, not that the thread had worn. At times, whatever noise she made, irritated. Paranoia set in. Even using the keyboard resonated in the early morning stillness, she hardly dare touch the keys. She hardly dared breath.

Ever since her husband's retirement in April she had not had the house to herself. A lot of the time she busied herself unnecessarily in the kitchen, folding and putting and emptying and filling and wiping and moving, all the time the intimacy of the radio distracting her, taking her on a journey of discovery in a world of her own, and always she was interrupted and it was turned off. Even in the car, the radio was turned off, or worse still changed to another station and even worse than that, a local station, harsh and loud, blasting in, making her jump, spoiling her listening and train of thought. It was impossible to follow anything without interruption. Looking through the wrong glasses she could see red squiggly lines on the screen, that were not there before, telling her that either her husband or her brother had changed the settings and until she had time to fiddle around and remove them, the glaring intrusions every fifteen minutes would have to stay. Not once had she been able to play *Madam Butterfly* at full volume, loud enough to shake the house and lift the roof tiles. Not once had she played The Doors so loud that she could not hear the purr of the car engine, the music escaping through open windows, feeling cool but not cool at all. Not once had she donned the walking boots and taken off at a brisk pace. Not once. In the end, she gave up.

Still reeling from the fallout, drifting and spinning around in the whirling solar system, her mind was unable to break free, she was finding it desperately hard to forgive. It would have been better to let rip and vent her simmering turmoil, say what she wanted and clear the air, but her anger bit deep, gnawing and hurting until the blood screamed through her veins trying to escape but was trapped by the knotty lump in her throat. Submerged, she was quiet and pensive, hostile to his attention. The pain and distress consumed and eroded, she thought of nothing else. Knowing full well the extent of his destruction, he could have ended it there and then and said sorry. But he didn't. Sorry, a simple word yet the hardest to say. The silence that had caused the stifling atmosphere in the first place suffocated. She wanted to scream.

Maybe it had been all her fault. Although she had not invited her brother to England, it had been her who had initially made contact and instigated the friendship. In the cold light of day, she should have let sleeping dogs lie.

Surprisingly, there were ragged tears in her oppressive sky, revealing clear blinks of blue that temporarily lifted her spirits.

Seeing her book on the shelf for the first time in the Stirling branch of Waterstones had to be a blink of blue. Such a long way from home, yet so much of *Patchwork* had been set there. Firstly she asked about it at the counter. The assistant typed in the title and up came three copies in stock. Scanning the bookshelves, she quickly found 'B'. There it was, the patchwork spine sandwiched tightly, ready to be picked up and devoured. A rich warm feeling consumed. Brimming with pleasure she removed it from the shelf and opened it, looking wildly at the pages near the front as though she had never seen them before. Turning it over, she read the back cover. Then she turned it back and looked at the front, her name and the title. Seeing her delight, the assistant came over and asked if she would sign the copies. Then, when she had, he promptly pressed a 'Signed by the author' sticker on the cover and turned the copies round to face the shop.

Earlier in the day, she had been at Stirling Castle and while she explored her favourite parts, her main purpose was to bequeath some artefacts to the museum. Off-loading her brother with a guided party, she made her way through the Regimental Museum to see the curator, explaining to Rod that she had a kilt, spats, cane, hats, jacket, etc. in the boot of her car. He was more than interested and the two of them walked purposefully across the Inner Close and the Outer Close back through the Forework and the Outer Defences to her car. Rod examined the kilt carefully, such a good example, pre-war, no, First World War. He gathered everything up. He was pleased and so was she. Glad to get rid of the memories, the cane forced between her shoulder blades in an effort to straighten her back, the false allusion forced on people when they saw her father wearing the full regalia, her mother blinded with what she thought was love even though he beat the shit out of her. She was not sorry to part with them. Understandably, no one in the family had wanted the garments. What use were they? She pictured them discarded to the tip when she had gone, crumpled and crushed and left to rot in a landfill site, fraying tartan and tattered ribbons exposed to the elements like the mangled scene of *The Thin Red Line* hanging in the museum. Mud and blood, gaping wounds, eagles and vultures swooping, their hooked beaks tearing into the bleeding carrion, picking over the decomposing bodies. Their historical value was worth more than that. She felt sure that by giving them to the museum, they would be appreciated. The one thing that was not being returned was the sporran and that left a sour note. Her brother had wanted it and what could she say? It didn't seem right that it was returning to the other side of the world. Her brother mothballed it and put it in the freezer ready to take home. She had met Rod before. He had pointed her in the right direction when she needed to know about her father's army record. He was passionate about his work. Leaving Stirling, the afternoon took her along the banks of Loch Lomond. The warm contented hills fringing the water's edge. The heathery mist wisping and drifting, lifting higher and higher, making way for the sun's golden warmth through the gaps in the cloud, dispersing the shiny wet on the road, dulling it to dry. Now and then there was a little rush of wind.

Seeing the gash of red span across the River Forth, was just breathtaking. It was such a feat of engineering. Just looking at it gave her strength. She took photos but none did it justice. She never tired of seeing it. Remembering the bridge since she was small, waiting in the grey light of morning to catch the first ferry at the end of the long, long journey from England. The pit stop to see an aunt in St Andrews was an old haunt. Stretching out, the West Sands, swimmers bravely enduring the cold North Sea and the methylated spirit coloured jellyfish. The Old Course unchanged, but the putting green reduced in size to accommodate a practice green for the rich and affluent. They had another pit stop in Perthshire to visit her cousin, before the long drive to Loch Ness. The scenery was majestic. Wild and wailing, she wanting her brother to see it in all its glory, so she drove. Seeing it from the car was not the same as walking in it as she had done a year ago with her son, breathing the same air as the plants, hearing the desolation. The horizon, a hazy aura, where the moors merged and blurred with the sky, leaping, tumbling rivers twisted and turned, tracks led to houses hidden from view, mystical turrets rose up through the trees, smoke curled in the still mythical air. The excellent meal at Dores Inn on the shore of Loch Ness was truly Scottish as was the welcoming accommodation in the rambling Ballindaroch House, reached by a dark overgrown track deep in the forest. Hadrian's Wall had to be included in the trip along with the Angel of the North so the next day, they slipped back into England via Northumberland. Skirting round the edge of Jedburgh, she remembered Helen. A phone call just before she left confirmed that Helen had died and that Pat, her sister was living in Spain. The sunny days ended abruptly as they approached Newcastle. The rain fell in one continuous grey metallic sheet. Meeting her niece was undoubtedly a blink of blue. Youth fuelled her energy and desire to show her aunt and uncle 'her' city, where she had chosen to settle, a far cry from the hamlet she grew up in. Her knowledge of which surpassed the irritation of the unfortunately named Jane bleating instructions on the 'sat-nav'. Unperturbed, she drove them into the city in all that terrible weather. They paddled up to their ankles crossing Grey Street to the restaurant. While they ate however, the rain eased and afterwards they walked along the Tyne to see the bridge so long imprinted in her mind. "The fog on the Tyne is all mine, all mine the fog on the Tyne is all mine." Although the light was dwindling and there was barely time they drove across the city to see the Angel of the North. How could she be there and not see it? The next day took them across the Pennines, stopping every now and then to photograph what was left of Hadrian's Wall. It vexed, that her husband's indifference had overshadowed and clouded her days. Papering over the cracks was difficult when it felt like the walls around her were crumbling.

The reason for the journey was that Donald had been born in Stirling, quite simply described on his birth certificate as Stirling Maternity Home. The eighteenth century Airthrey Castle was now the School of Law and part of the University Campus but in the years between 1935 and 1965 it had been used as a maternity home. After a long detour through the grounds they came across the imposing building. Built of stone it stood steadfast and defiant, its weathered frontage softened by the sweep of tended beds and landscaping, impeccably maintained, the soil, a fine dark tilth and in true Scottish municipal land management, not a weed in sight. They found themselves in a dimly lit tiled entrance hall. A short flight of stairs led upwards but Donald was happy enough to stand where his mother would have come in 1946, to listen to her screams and cries as she delivered him into the world. They turned from the dimness of the hallway to normality on the other side of the great oak door. There was no place on earth like Scotland and she was pleased to show it off to her half-brother, just as their father had shown his mother.

Her friends, knowing how she needed some TLC organised afternoon tea at Teapots. In spite of it being a rainy afternoon, it temporarily lifted her spirits. Teapots had once been a cottage, its black glass panelled door opened directly onto the high street. The front room and the back room had been converted to one and arranged with a scattering of tables, square blue polyester cloths thrown over white and chairs, like church hall chairs arranged in twos and fours. There were four chairs with wipeable plastic drop-ins. She would have found it difficult to sit on one of those and fortunately, she didn't have to. Telescopic umbrellas lay sodden under them or hooked on the backs, quietly dripping into the busy dark blue carpet. Not surprisingly there was a musty choking smell of clinging damp hanging in the air. The carpeting muffled steps and the sound of scraping chairs and hid deep in its stunted pile a multitude of spills and stains. The smell and the chairs made her a little apprehensive but bravely she chose her favourite from the menu, egg and cress sandwiches, coffee and walnut cake from the selection of cakes that took pride of place in the glass cabinet, followed by strawberries and cream. Sadly, it did not come up to her expectation, it was meagre and tasteless, the bread indifferent, the cress lacked vim and the egg was egg, nothing more. Nursing her tea she could never understand why people got worked up about a Victoria sandwich or indeed any variation of it, praising its merits, its lightness, its texture. The strawberries and cream were insipid, served in a sundae glass that had seen better days. She did not feel appreciative, her senses were magnified, her hidden agenda tainting her usual sunny outlook, seeing the worst. While she ate and talked with her friends, enjoying their company, her eyes travelled round the room, an emporium of Olney quaintness. Three ducks flew low, flush to the wall. Had the clock stopped before the war or after the war? She was no longer a fan of memorabilia but the clutter distracted from the dowdy colour scheme, the municipal green and beige was relieved with a gallery of pictures, each the cover of an old magazine mounted in a frame. An assortment of teapots occupied ledges and sills gathering dust. Seven glass lampshades hung from the ceiling, each suspended on three chains that attached to a hook on the ceiling rose. They discussed how they used to be the fashion. Each pearly opal bowl was different, marbled and mottled, pebbled and feathered in 'mother of the bride' confections. Every now and then the bell over the door jangled brightly temporarily breaking into the classical music playing in the background, disturbing the murmuring hum. Lorries, as wide as the street rumbled passed in a low gear, plates clattered. There should have been a by-pass years ago, but nobody wanted it in their back yard. She had a grand design for one, a sweeping span of steel arches four miles long, across the Ouse valley. People would come from miles around to see the work of art, to admire its slender frame, its strength and beauty.

Sometimes she played putting on her own and felt

overwhelmingly skittish when she putted a hole-in-one on the garden putting green. An amused smile broke her concentration and moving rapidly, like a child, almost skipped to retrieve the ball from the flowerpot, buried flush with the grass.

She delighted in culinary matters, the meanest tear rolling onions with their tight white bulbs, the comforting warmth of ripening tomatoes, the summery fragrance. August. The robust earthy smell of a bowl of borsch, its startling deep red colour, her hands stained pink and sink splattered and the mossy mini eco-worlds that lived on top of the beetroots jostling for position in the tightly packed rows across the garden. Apart from her husband objecting to domestic noises, nothing was too much trouble. Even simple tasks were a pleasure. Making a cake, which she called 'the very good orange cake' because it was, filled her with pleasure, each crumb, perfect, soft and moist with ground almonds and it didn't matter that it wasn't finished in delicate orange glace icing. Waiting for it to cool, the friendly smell permeating the entire house, was too inviting. It just had to be cut. She lost track of all the meals prepared and eaten. The endless cups of tea and pots of coffee made.

Besides reading she wrote things down, jotted randomly in her lovely notebook. It was a means of speaking without being heard. Although not good with clever words, it was a way of describing in detail things that she thought about or had experienced, or memories that had got lost in the crowded days of living, bringing them back to life. She could not possibly say these things because people would think she was mad. Maybe she was. It would seem ridiculous to describe a cake as the 'very good orange cake' or the disturbing, intimidating whirl of the helicopter blades, the frightening hovering noise, like that in *The Deer Hunter* when the people were so desperate to leave Saigon. Likewise the menacing threat, deep in the ground when a combine harvester rumbled past, worse still, at night when the great hulking shape loomed out of the darkness, its piercing lights, perched high, throwing scary shadows or the roast potatoes making sparrow noises in the oven or a kick of Marmite or a gang of skateboards growling on the footpath opposite, grating on the nerves, annoying the neighbourhood, or the distant droning echo of a motorbike on the bypass, making the earth shiver, the sound going on and on, vibrating in her head long after it was gone. A glass of wine lubricated her inhibitions and she was free to be herself. Even after a sip she was slightly off centre and no longer afraid of her imagination or lost for words, her writing was fluid, effortlessly pouring onto the page. There was no pressure. Her frustration came when she fought to remember and retain words in her head, repeating them all the time until she had a moment to write them down. Days and weeks later she would come across her tightly folded secrets on scraps of paper buried amongst the fluff and debris in the depths of her pockets. Anyone else coming across them would assume them to be rubbish or feel ashamed that they had come across something that was private, hastily folding them again. More often than not however, something more vital would intrude, interrupting her train of thought, the word escaping once more. Writing down her harboured thoughts was liberating, freeing-up time for the present. She saw it as a voice, for people like her who were silenced. There was so much to engross her, the unfurling silk of the pool, the sulphur yellow sky. No. If she talked as she thought, people would think she was mad. It was best to say nothing. Writing her thoughts in her head, she withdrew into the shadow and silence prevailed.

THE OUTBURST

Feeling empty she had gone off to the shops for some retail therapy and on returning home, found her husband sorting photographs. He had laid them out across the kitchen table. He had been searching for one in particular and was pleased that he had come across it. Some were black and white and some were colour and except for a few all were square. She stared blindly at the school photo taken over fifty years ago. Her eyes scanned the rows of shabby children, girls with plaits, boys in braces and short trousers, their eyes squinting in the sunlight. The picture had been taken on the school playing field, in the background was the orchard where more recently her mother's bungalow had been built.

"I can't see me." She said, squinting at the picture. "Perhaps I will with a magnifying glass." Her husband produced the magnifying glass. She hovered it slowly over the faces. "I still can't see me. I must be off the picture on the end of a row." It was no big deal. He thought or maybe liked to think that she was the little girl in the front row, sitting cross-legged, her chin resting in her hands. It wasn't her. She looked too pretty and her plaits were looped, she didn't remember wearing her plaits like that. Anyway she looked like a boy, plain. Quite what happened next came as a complete shock. Her heart quickened. His face became rigid and his eyes and the frowning scars between were fierce. Mercilessly hissing and spitting feathers he snarled and showed his fangs. It was a murderous look. He unleashed a scathing attack. Expletives and a plethora of scornful abuse ignited flames of stinging septic scorn and splintering glass. He was seething and loathed the very sight of her. He calmed. His withering ice-cold look despised her. She did not recognize him. Awash with tears she stared in disbelief. Unwavering, she confronted him, protesting why he was so aggressive. By pushing the boundaries however, she had overstepped the mark and pushed him too far. As quickly as the volatile exchange started, tears and silence extinguished the fire. He stopped speaking. For the rest of the day she was ostracized and he sulked, totally ignoring her, even refusing to be in the same room as her. Full of heady emotion, her mind swam. Time stood still. Over and over the voices in her head replayed the scene. Where would she go? Why would she leave? What would she say? On and off throughout the day her eyes watered uncontrollably, the relentless tide of tears was too great to be blinked away, they spilled and washed over her cheeks. Her heart ached. Without his deep dependable love there was nothing. The immense gulf left an unfathomable emptiness. For some reason, in her head she was singing 'I vow to thee my country' until her lungs became choked and her voice quivered, becoming nothing more than an inaudible whimper to be reduced further to a breathy jerky hum, eventually leaving Jupiter to play somewhere. She left the world behind. '… and the Universe begins to ring and resound. It is no longer human voices. It is Planets and suns revolving in their orbits.' Beleaguered, she broke down. Drained, the bitter onslaught left her exhausted. Smothered sobs and tears of regret seeped into her pillow until sleep drowned her sorrow.

When your heart is black and broken
And you need a helping hand
When you're so much in love
You don't know just how much you can stand
When your questions go unanswered
And the silence is killing you
Take my hand baby, I'm your man
I've got love enough for two.

Living, as she felt on a fault line, the eventual tsunami was to be expected. However strong they were it would jolt and slip to uproot and displace her. Torn from her moorings the dark black water closed over her head. Left adrift to survive in the perilous sea, she slipped below the surface. Her flailing arms and cries for help went unnoticed. A tide of biblical proportion spewed before her, pushing out of reach all that she held dear. Memories swam before her as the giant wave left behind a wash of catastrophic devastation in her mind. And although she was still breathing, she was numb. Nothing made any sense. Her hopes had been shattered and her dreams crushed. Like a severed limb she had been left to bleed. All around, the emaciated destruction left her feeling bewildered and isolated, uncertain of anything.

Liberation came when she returned to work in September. Three months had passed, her precious summer gone. Floundering, she clutched to the routine of the new term, knowing that the busy days would crowd her mind and in time a sense of proportion would return.

Mike, in Waterstones must have thought, oh God, no, it's that woman, when she approached. There were apologies and lame excuses for not contacting her and to make amends, there and then the book signing was arranged. Two weeks later when 'foot-fall' was at its busiest she stood watching the customers drifting in, in peaks and troughs, her weight on one leg and then the other. She encouraged two book sales and apparently that was good. Authors often sold none. Some people purchased a whole armful of books, some took advantage of the special offer of, buy two get one free situated at the entrance to the store but most people who wondered in, bought nothing, they just followed like sheep. Breaking the monotony, she walked around, randomly browsing through the books as though she was a customer. Many had been best sellers but on reading the first page she decided that they were not better than her book that she was trying to promote and unless it was brought to people's attention it would sit on a warehouse shelf gathering dust. With renewed vigour she composed a letter and sent it along with a copy from her stockpile of books to the daily papers. Just the thought of an acknowledgement either by post or email kept her going.
Two weeks later a reply from the *Daily Mail* arrived saying that as they received 300 books a week, and that space was limited to twenty books and that it was impossible to review her book. Rejection. Crest-fallen but not discouraged she sent the returned book out again enclosing a determined

letter politely insisting that it should be reviewed, and so that he didn't have to read the entire book she drew his attention to page fifty-three in particular, implying that the whole story hinged on that page. Being quietly modest, the hard hitting, direct-sell was not her, but she had nothing to lose and she was always hopeful, it was early days, it was the time of the year, she must be patient and wait.

The fabric of the land was changing. In a matter of weeks golden fields turned brown with the plough were carpeted with splinters of green. The trees turned to gold then brown in the Indian summer. In cheerful bursts the mischievous leaves scurried this way and that, blindly rushing about, they chattered and laughed as they scampered around in the wind, eddying and swirling, gathering momentum, only to have their fun brought to an abrupt stop against the fence. The perfume of burning wood scented the autumn air. With their leaves lost, the black bones of trees stood naked against the pomegranate sky. Filtering through their charcoal fretwork she could see the early morning traffic going about its business and the orange glow of streetlights, evenly spaced. The indulgent sky cast a haunting light, an enchanting light, illuminating what was usually hidden by the undergrowth. It came flooding through the leafless canopy. The wide screen, high definition gaping sky was full of promise, she wanted to gulp it down. On such mornings her journey to school was too short.

Shadows slanted in the shallow winter sun. Long and lean, her own, stretched out across the pavement.

The maelstrom had abated. The armistice was sealed in a present of perfume. Really, she had no need to doubt, but she couldn't help feeling guarded against his rough tongue and impatient voice. The door still closed when she flicked the switch on the vacuum cleaner. For her, shoring-up and restoring what they had from the rubble was going to take time.

She came home to a solitary man who had nothing much to say for himself, his face slack, sitting wedged in the corner of the settee opposite the television, his arms crossed over his chest and his hands clamped in his oxters to keep them warm and near enough the window to see out if he levered himself up. Sometimes there was a foreign smell, a sour stale lingering odour that she couldn't quite place and cups stained brown with endless cups of tea, made for the sake of it, made out of boredom and lack of company. Men at home with time on their hands had no shape to their day. They didn't see windows to clean and washing to iron. He traipsed in and out to the garage, treading sodden leaves and grit into the house. His cheerless days were too long and hers were too short. Between breaths, with no time to waste, she dove-tailed chores and shopping, cooking and activities in order to get the most from her weekends. Originally she was going to do the weekly shop but a last minute decision to indicate left meant that she was going home. She justified the change, she was tired, it was dark, it was wet, it would be busy, she had already made the dinner, there was milk and she would go first thing in the morning before the rush when she was fresh. With her extra time she went for a swim and washed her hair. By 8.15 a.m. the next morning she was piling the all too heavy bags into the boot of her car. The whole day lay ahead. But she frittered it and dithered about doing nothing very much, ending up feeling annoyed with herself. If she was honest she knew the reason for her indifference. Inside, her discomfort continued to fester, anxiety slowly decomposing, quietly eating away, to manifest itself like some awful rotting canker.

A failure on her part as with other times in her life, she was not prepared for the next phase, old age. Refusing to admit that she was old, believing that she could still climb mountains, she would never give in, throw in the towel and call it a day. Accepting it would take the rest of her life and she planned on living a very long time.

It seemed that she had known her husband all her life and

presumed that they both chased the same dreams. Now retired however, her husband readily resigned himself, insisting that he was old and his easy acceptance maddened her. Indeed, at times he seemed old, especially when the melancholy winter months took hold and the cold weather set in with what seemed unending dull drab days of creeping gloom or rain splattered days or raw complaining windy days and he was restricted to being indoors, hibernating in the dreary half-light, closed off from the world, shuffling around the furniture in his slippers. Without her company time weighed heavily. Not knowing whither to feel sorry for him or annoyed with him, his dour face looked pinched and futile. Vegetating, with only the television for company he became obsessed with the weather and tracked the progress of the fronts and the pressure, flicking from channel to channel for the very latest frenetic updates and when she got in from work she listened as he reported to her about the chaos on the roads in their region that scrolled down the right hand side of the screen, or the below zero temperature in Novosibirsk a million miles away, or accidents in an isolated village in Norfolk, or a fatality involving a motorbike, or, even when the weather was good, a lorry on its side on a slip road or a roundabout. "Did he slip on the ice? No, he was going too fast." Tutting. "Professional drivers." His concern about the shortage of rain became a talking point. The water table was not being replenished. There was no flow in the river. "We need some rain." He would say. It was sweeping but really he had a jaundiced outlook on life, having little or nothing good to say about anything. It was not a cheery welcome when she came home. It was selfish, but really she only cared about her family and friends and after a busy day at work, the state of the motorway was not high on the agenda. In the sudden isolation that he found himself in, she supposed that seeking refuge with the TV was his way of staying in touch with the wider world, like a safety blanket. At least he would have something to say to her when she walked through the door. In stereo, Radio 2 would be on in the dining room and he would stand between the two rooms listening to the radio while watching the TV and he would tell her when she got in from work, about the latest round on Pop-master and how the contestant rambled on and on about nothing and wanted to say hello to all and sundry. On the settee beside him, he powered the TV and controlled the temperature of the entire house. One day, when she had moved the thermostat to a colder place, in order to maintain some level of heat, he appeared and questioned where it was. Alarmed, colour drained from her face. Dread dropped like a stone to the pit of her stomach, claiming that it must have fallen down the side of the chair, quickly pulling the cushions away to find it. Sure enough. "Here it is." She said, by the skin of her teeth. Sometimes, when she was truly cold to the core, she would open the airing cupboard door, where the 'advance heat' control was housed and press the button. Straight away her husband would know as the sound of hot water coursed through the veins of the house, maybe, even before that, as the door rubbed against the pile of the carpet as she opened it. She had rarely held the two remote control devices and hardly knew how to change channels on the TV. It was generally her husband who decided what they watched. That didn't mean to say that they didn't enjoy programmes together, but it was him who made the final decision, saying that, if she wanted, she could watch TV in the other room. He was easily exasperated over nothing, becoming anxious and irritated, if someone parked outside 'his' house when they were expecting visitors, continually checking to see if the car had gone. And never more than when a silver soft topped sports car. parked for a month, hoping that when he contacted the police that it would be removed. How he objected to someone else making use of 'his' space. It was not a cheap alternative to a long-stay car park. Like a nosey neighbour he would look out on to the road, watching the comings and goings, stretching up out of his seat, craning his neck to see a car pull up or standing in the bay window, hands deep in the softness of his jogging bottoms pockets, contemplating, turning to the left and to the right, complaining to no-one that there was a thirty mile speed limit and he would tell her when she came home from work about the postman deliberately stepping over the flowerpot or the man, who, when walking his dog, he observed, did not carry a poo bag. Sometimes it was like coming home to a dishevelled old man, unkempt, his hair this way and that, his face unshaven. It felt like she was no longer his lover, but someone functional and useful. She felt like his carer. She felt like her mother. She didn't have to see a trail of toast crumbs to know he hadn't used a plate, she could feel them on the sole of her slippers, her leather Moroccan slippers, stained-red in a vat of ox-blood, haggled for, in the heat of the moment in the souk in Agadir, wearing them like the locals with the backs pressed firmly down. Cooking was not his forte and her husband would forage in the fridge and graze on nothing very much. Doing his bit for his bank account and global warming he became pre-occupied with shutting doors and would go around the house turning off lights, and switching off sockets believing it to conserve energy. Having a water meter installed was his next economy and duly phoned and made arrangements. Talking with friends, being on one could half the yearly bill. Having a bath became a thing of the past as did flushing the toilet. He was not put off by acrid yellow water fermenting and discolouring the bowl. She found the wreaking stagnating smell of a cow shed disgusting and continued to flush normally, randomly checking and flushing like a toilet attendant. In the garden, an army of water butts stood to attention, like sentries on watch, guarding the down pipes. As part of the lengthy irrigation system, buckets and containers were placed strategically to capture what fell from the sky, decanting and saving the precious resource for another day. With nothing much to do her husband rummaged around finding pictures that he had forgotten about and she had put in store, out of sight, leaning in the gaps between the walls and cupboards. Finding picture hooks and a hammer, he hung them around the house. She said nothing. At the first opportunity she would remove them and banish them to the charity shop for good. Likewise with the ornaments fished out and arranged, they too would go. Where he didn't like her books, written, as he said, by those born with silver spoons in their mouths, he turned their spines to the wall. Most days he was bright enough, but it wasn't enough for a proud man, a proud working man. He knew it.

Like her mother in her old age, he closed the curtains and pulled down the blinds before it was dark. Once, when calling in on her mother, she remembered her drawing the sitting room curtains when the sun was still hanging in the pink afternoon. "But it's still light." She protested. "How can you shut out the light?" flinging the curtains open again. Her mother's face turned ugly. Dutifully she closed them again, kissed her on the cheek and left, leaving her sitting in the gloom. Sometimes, she and her husband went to the nearest pub and at a certain time the curtains would be removed from their tie-backs and drawn. For a moment her body tightened. She wanted to say, "Please don't shut them." But how could she? How could she say that she wanted to see the sky between the houses, to see the fuzzy slice of moon or the rain or the man walking his dog, his head tucked into his upturned collar of his puffer jacket, that she knew smelled of frying because it had hung on the nail on the back door. Nursing her glass of wine she wanted to line up the drainpipe with the wall and the doorframe and the windows of the terraced cottages opposite and marvel, Victorians did all that without sophistication, wearing collars with studs, hob-nailed boots and smoking pipes. How could she say? She wanted to see what was going on. There was something that she didn't like about closing out the world, about feeling trapped. If she went in after the curtains had been closed, her anxiety was lessened and concluded that it was the ritual of closing them that bothered her.

The ground shivered in the last of the light. Another three months had passed.

It was hard keeping it all together, pretending, wanted to say something, but not wanting to rock the boat and spoil the harmony. The time was never right. Sometimes she was downcast and seemed withdrawn. At times she was so far away, she didn't feel part of his life. Estranged, she didn't feel that she belonged. She felt as though she was visiting from some distant far away place. Well practised, she was good at hiding her feelings, not moody, not complaining or annoyed, not tired, not angry, not anything really. False. Being busy disguised her wretchedness. So used to the emptiness she wondered at times who her true self was.

Since childhood she had spent her entire life fostering uncomfortable traits. It was the only way to get by, pretending to have courage instead of escaping into sadness, giving a false impression. She had learnt from her downtrodden mother, who too, had spent most of her life weighed down with oppression and festering guilt, admitting to no-one, her dreadful experiences, forever silenced like haunting war time memories cast into the vaults deep in the back of her mind. All the time cowering like a frightened animal caught in the dazzle of glaring headlights. Only in later life had she sought redemption and took to visiting the sick and the housebound, sometimes taking homemade soup or a small jar of homemade raspberry jam or like a disciple tended the feet of the parishioners, even though her podiatry skills were rudimentary or fattened their pillows to make them comfortable. Pretending to have courage had been her coping mechanism as well. Both had lived a tangle of lies and suspicion, hypocrisy and secrecy and unlike her mother who lost the will in the end and left it too late to do anything about it, she longed for her conscience to be free of the wretched baggage that had accumulated over the years. She was sick of the deceit and pretence. Even waiting at the chancel steps on the brink of the rest of her life she was not convinced when the vicar read,
"Therefore if any man can shew any just cause, why they may not lawfully be joined together, let him now speak, or else hereafter for ever hold his peace."
Followed by,
"I require and charge you both, as ye will answer at the dreadful day of judgement when the secrets of all hearts shall be disclosed, that if either of you know any impediment, why ye may not be lawfully joined together in matrimony, ye do

now confess it. For be ye well assured, that so many as are coupled together otherwise than God's word doth allow are not joined together by God ; neither is their matrimony lawful." that someone in the congregation would not leap to their feet and declare the whole event as null and void. The certainty of anything seemed precarious and it left her feeling wary and sceptical of people, regarding them with distrust. What she had really wanted was to be married in secret, in another place, where nobody knew her, but the need to justify her ideas was too daunting. How could she have explained?

Then there were times when they unexpectedly took themselves out for a drink or found themselves alone in the house, sharing a bottle of wine, talking and smiling, laughing, breaking the silence, a crucial few minutes in time, when everything stood still. Captured. How she treasured those moments before another gulp or another sip rendered tiredness, blurring the brief comfortable atmosphere, the poison clouding and staining, merging the edges of words, so that they were no longer defined. Sleep. By the morning those precious words in those precious moments were forgotten. The dreams and promises meant nothing. She needed time. There was never enough. It was like an act, and for different scenes she would change her clothes and learn new lines. How she was at school was entirely different. A fly on the wall, not that she would want a fly on the wall, at school would see a different person, assertive and confident and she liked to think, respected. With her children, she was herself and sometimes when they sat around the table as a family, she was herself. But alone with her husband there were long unbearable silences, partly because she couldn't speak and partly because he had nothing to say. A long time ago when they were young she used to say to him, (it was a girl thing). "What are you thinking about?" Shifting shadows etched his face. Dismissive and defensive, and a bit irritated as though she had no right to pry into his soul, he replied. "I'm not thinking about anything." He didn't off-load his thoughts and let her in. He didn't let her turn over the stones to see the resentment, the confusion or even the joy in his streaming mind. From what he had said over the years in those precious moments of time, she gleaned only a thin spread of childhood. Always a listener, she was interested. It was what made him how he was. She was attracted to his foreignness. It was probably why he searched for answers in the cumbersome books that he read, new titles reviewed and brought to his attention on the radio and the newspapers, factual evidence about people's lives in his parent's country during and before the war, researched in depth and only recently coming to light. He lusted after information, eager to find anything, a link or a name, something to get hold of and call it his. In the books he found himself placing his parents in the humble villages deep in the Steppes going about their day or trudging deep in mud, slipping, trying to stay upright, rifle butts to their heads, starvation imminent. Often infused in self-pity he regretted not knowing until now. Absorbed, he blotted up the words, sometimes reading aloud to her or describing how it was, wishing he had asked about their lives before they died, feeling guilty for not having done so. How contented she felt when she fell asleep and he was there sat, bolstered against the pillows at the side of her, reading until the pictures of 'his' past faded and he too fell asleep. It did at times make her sad that he dished out his deep-rooted stubbornness on his children, her children too. Hurt, when he declined to help his father on the computer, her son took himself off to another chair, away from his father and then when her husband thought he would involve him in catching fish from the pond in the garden, he moved indoors, leaving him to it. Digging his heals in, a dark mood set in and silence fell. Lasting unresolved scars of frustration and rejection, had never allowed him to develop a coping mechanism for being refused or denied, which surprised her. Brought up, often starved of the barest necessities she would have thought he would have been more resilient. He confessed only the other day to never being given a football. She wanted to go out there and then and buy one. And although in deprivation, a football was hardly a necessity, to a five year old as passionate as him, it was more important than eating.

He was the second of three children, all the time fighting to be heard, fighting for recognition, his brother and his sister crowding him out, his sister simply because she was a girl and his brother because he was the clever one and didn't compare. Once he left school, his goal was to 'better' himself, materially and financially, saving and securing and safeguarding a better life for himself and ultimately his family.

Although she did at times, she didn't want to feel sorry for him and she didn't want him to feel sorry for her. It was difficult to break the silence. What she wanted to do was talk, but she knew that she lacked the language to express what she wanted to say. She wanted to talk quietly and softly about those things under the stones, to have a meaningful conversation, to get past the stunted clumsy politeness of strangers, to rekindle the embers before the fire finally died, not to be theatrical or neurotic, not to rant and rage, not to raise voices, not to argue but to listen to each other, not to lose control. But she knew that she would not be convincing, her voice becoming high and hysterical. He would not listen to her and within moments, the pitch would change, each would be defensive, hissing their venom and spitting their anger, each backing up their case with ammunition and hurtling it until she was wavering, weak and shaking with fear, her face flushed and her eyes itchy and swollen with a rush of tears. The impending danger of compromising what she had, had always stopped her. Too afraid of the consequences, she was fearful of failure, frightened of getting it wrong, unable to go back. Trying to draw it out of him, would, she knew, take days, weeks even. It was too much to risk. He might turn sour. She had known other times when he had been equally as hurtful and eventually pushed it to the back of her mind. Once, she remembered composing a list of her grievances and handed him the piece of paper. Barely glancing at it, he screwed it into a tight ball and threw it back at her, drawing her attention instead to a complete stranger carrying a heavy bag, not seeing that she too carried a heavy bag, that she too, had bruises on her arms. Those close to him went unnoticed. Finding a letter written by him to her in their teens confirmed that he hadn't changed. It was a letter of apology. He had spoken out-of-turn and hurt her feelings and the letter was trying to make amends. Even then she had worried about those sudden outbursts but had always stuck up for him, forgiven him, set him on a pedestal, found reasons for abruptness, made allowances for rudeness and excuses for intolerance.

From her schoolgirl crush she had lost her heart to him in 1966. Even before then, when she was eleven and he was thirteen she set her heart on him. He was tall and broad-shouldered, he was as seductively dark as she was fair and he was handsome and simply a glimpse of him in the corridor lining up for science, or watching him, dreamy-eyed at lunchtime playing tennis kept her going. Nobody else compared (or had come remotely close since). Knowing the crowd that he went around with she was convinced that he was unobtainable. And being plain and ordinary, she certainly did not feature in his day. She was just a silly little third year. That however, did not stop her being totally in awe of the boy that came into her life. From a distance she admired and adored him, for four years she idolized him. Then by chance one day she went to his house with his sister and he was there. She swooned when she saw him, her heart leapt like a licking, leaping flame and her legs turned to jelly and when he acknowledged her and said hello she was totally consumed and found it difficult to hide the trembling palpitations that reached the furthest extremities. It was the beginning of the rest of her life. Only a short time later he said that he loved her. Believing him, it was surely the first time anyone had said that to her. Until then she had not been aware of being loved.

Throughout her childhood she felt that she was nothing but a darned nuisance, an inconvenience, better seen and not heard and being sent to a home was a frequent threat when her parents had had enough. Failed love. Not until the end of her life in the elegance of the green room overlooking the garden, did her mother press her bony freckled hand over hers and say "I love you." Did she just say that or was it, as she got older, a notion that came into her head, worrying and gnawing at her memories, that things are or were better or worse than they used to be, embroidered and embellished to fool even herself? In her old age did she dwell on times past, remembering the shame of finding herself in the mother and baby home, then, in stark contrast, the elation that followed when her daughter was born, filtering out the awfulness and the consequence of a rash fumble with a man who had seduced his way into her life and in her naivety had been flattered by his attention, infatuated by his charm, seeing only the special distant moments and the here and now, making her mostly miserable life bearable? And would she have said it to her had she not been successful, because she saw striving for an education and career as a means to a better life and social mobility, a life better than the one she had been dealt? And although she loved and was immensely proud of her grandchildren, photos littered the sills, she did not consider her own daughters' sowing and reaping and having a string of them between them was anything to go by. It just made for hardship and multiplied the workload and decreased the opportunities. Only occasionally did she see her daughters as a source of joy and pleasure. She envied families who had their children's interest at heart, like her dearest friend who simply adored her father and just oozed with love when she spoke of him, unlike her and her sister who seemed to bring themselves up, only realizing that they had done something wrong when they were reprimanded with a voice like a 'whetted knife'. It was a loveless upbringing. Arguments and back-biting would break out or unforgiving silences grew increasingly hostile. And maybe meeting this boy of her dreams had saved her from what, a life like her mother's or perhaps something even worse.

They spent their first few months getting to know each other – sharing – walking - talking – occasionally they kissed, innocent sweet honeyed kisses. They lay, her on her back, him hoisted on his elbow, tenderly taking her in, undisturbed on the baked chalky earth, hidden deep in the long waving summer grass, the hum of insects, nodding harebells and springy ladies-bedstraw, water crowfoot buoyant, drifting in the current, overhead, clouds bubbled and dispersed. It didn't rain or if it did, it was the lightest, softest rain or sudden bursting rain when they ran giggling and damp to take shelter beneath the beech trees, either way they didn't notice. They listened to their favourite music on crackly stations on her small leather bound transistor radio. He wore a suit and tie and was chivalrous and courteous and when they crossed the road he lightly took her arm and gently ushered her from one side of the pavement to the other insisting that he walked on the wild side, protecting her from the dangers that lay beyond the kerb. He was honourable and she never doubted his integrity. Over time their tender slow burning affection blossomed. Wrapped and absorbed in their heart breaking devotion for each other, they were selfishly unaware of anyone else. Their hearts beat as one. Her wildest dreams had come true. Not wanting to loose or spoil her good fortune, she locked her secrets away, knowing that they would in time, return to haunt her. And so, right from the very beginning the tangle of deceit and lies was embedded and continued, just like it had for her mother. Had she too been infatuated, swept-along by his swarthy complexion and weathered gypsy look, elevating to everything that followed? Had she been gullible and hasty? She should have stopped to think it through. From the beginning she should have been honest, but the possibility of losing him was too great and she did not want him to feel that he had been gullible and manipulated. In his youth he was attentive and generous and when separated, they wrote letters daily, yearning for each other. He loved everything about her, her innocence, her sensitivity, her reserved demureness, her lingering shyness, her voice, her laugh, her smooth bare face, so many things. He made her feel special and wanted. His love for her was intoxicating. She was deliriously happy.

AND NOW

Only the other day she leapt from the white leather settee in the hairdressers where she was waiting for the quarterly trim when she saw his passing reflection. Immediately she rushed to the door and called. On hearing his name he turned and smiled, retracing his steps back to her. Still she melted at the sight of her handsome husband. Like magnetic poles they were drawn towards each other, even if they caught sight of each other when driving, they would flash their lights and wave, or if they met-up somewhere other than home, a deep velvet warmth spread between them, being away from her for twenty four hours, he saw her in a new light.

Truly believing that her blinding love would last forever she completely overlooked the fact that she would change. Having held on to his darkness for nearly fifty years, not seeing his greying hair, not seeing his thickening waist or his slowing pace and increasing lethargy she was saddened by the gathering bitterness that she felt. Until now she had thrived on his dry humour and quirky ways, his spontaneity, his infectious laugh and his slow teasing smile. Still waters ran deep. They had kept her going. How she ached for the beauty that they once shared, for the taste of love. She could imagine what he would say. As she knew he would be, he was totally in denial, unaware of the terrible hurt he had caused, too close to see her despair. He had tunnel vision. He was dismissive and shrugged her off. "I'm only joking." He said. "You make a fuss out of nothing." Or he implied that she had overreacted or imagined and inflated his irrational behaviour, misinterpreting what he had said. She had exaggerated and made a mountain out of a molehill and blown what he had said out of all proportion. Apportioning blame, he refused to admit that he was wrong. She might as well accept the fact. He was infallible. Even when they had arranged to meet outside Lloyds bank, when he had been to his bank and her to the post office, he brushed aside the fact that she had waited for him for over an hour. Standing, glued to the spot, out of the drizzly rain under the awning of the Indian restaurant next door, she was aware of the church bells chiming on the quarter, of people on their lunch-break, getting a coffee or having some chips, the constant flow of people going in the bank and into the betting office, cars stopping at the crossing, of the most enormous green transporter full of livestock which undoubtedly had been directed wrongly by the 'sat-nav' and a man opposite who, when the rain stopped stood outside his card shop, his hands in his pockets. A couple of times she put up the umbrella and walked the few yards to the corner just to see if she could see him. Had he forgotten, or met a friend or got cornered into opening another account (which was unlikely) she could have understood but to turn round and walk home when they had arranged to meet was beyond her. Other things contributed to his sullen behaviour to which she bore the brunt. The finality of never going to work again had to sink in and he had to adapt to the change in routine with the dark winter months ahead. Retirement was not the round yellow sun in the big blue sky, a neat brick house with a picket fence and a garden gate, apples on the tree. At times it was dull and boring. At times it was lonely. The long friendless days stretched out. Trying to occupy them was a task in itself. Nothing that he did used up as much time as going to work. Even hobbies that he had longed to spend more time on did not fill the hours. The new life was different. For over forty years he had been synchronized and programmed to work. The grinding repetitiveness of the regime had left its mark. To suddenly and it seemed suddenly be removed from the workplace, to have time to choose when and where and how and what, was proving difficult. He no longer featured on the radar, no longer a useful member of society, no longer increasing productivity, smelling of inks and chemicals, his hands ingrained, no longer earning and providing which once filled him with pride. He had lost his purpose. Almost overnight he had become moribund, worthless, no longer useful to anyone, fit for nothing. Depressingly redundant. Already cantankerous, he would suit being old. People would make the assumption that his awkwardness and irritability was to be expected because he was old and make allowances, unaware that he had always been like that. Nothing more than an easterly wind could tip the balance. Querulous and grumpy, he was unable to cope with imperfections. Knots of pain gnawed, preventing sleep and he was increasingly frustrated by Dupuytren's Contracture that was deforming and impairing the function of his hands, his precious hard working hands, his big strong hands that rubbed her back and held her close. Over time, as his hands were gradually closing she found herself doing things for him or leaving things ready so that he didn't have to struggle. Constantly he was reminded as the movement of his hands became awkward and clumsy like a clawing grapnel, feeling robbed of their tactile feeling. He could not remove from his mind the grim faced officer at immigration control when he couldn't flatten his hand on the x-ray machine. Holding his hands in hers, she carefully turned them over. The deformed tendons settled in his palm like sleeping snakes. His little fingers, rigid and inert. The symptoms were hereditary and he felt guilty about not knowing if his father had been inflicted. Over the years he had paid his father little attention, rarely asking him how he felt, ignoring the obvious degeneration, let alone checking his palms. On broaching the subject, he stiffened like the tendons in his hands. He stood like his father, when randomly looking out the kitchen window, one slippered foot slightly in front of the other, his lumbering arms hanging loosely, the cup of his hand turned towards his back, his fingers curled as tough he was going to wheel a barrow.

Another irritation was that their son had returned home 'temporarily'. Oil and water never did mix without an emulsifier and that was her, trying her best to smooth things over. Their son seriously needed to think long and hard about how he had become. His arrogance and his callous unforgivable rudeness was inexcusable. He would flounce through the house at a hundred miles an hour, big strides covering the distance between the front door and the back, his saccharine face hiding a veil of bottled-up resentment. As if they didn't know he was there. Deliberately, he would come to the table when his parents had practically finished eating, his food cold, congealed and moulded to the plate, so avoiding conversation and when he had finished, he would push his plate away, and without fail, leave a statutory morsel on the side and his chair not tucked in. His trademarks. He didn't say hello. He didn't say goodbye. Few could penetrate his brick-wall defiance and his bitterness whipped up now and then, leaving a desolate face. Questions went unanswered. And if he spoke, which he sometimes did, he mumbled and what he said was barely audible. He was hard work. He was cool with his mates, who sat low in their low cars and drove off with the door still open, one hand on the wheel. He needed to think long and hard about the people he was hurting, his insensitivity, his lack of respect, and his cruel disregard for people's feelings, especially her husband's. Paradoxically, even though it was sometimes justly deserved she couldn't bear her son to be rude to him, but at the same time admiring his courage to be confrontational and stand his ground. Even though she loathed his behaviour, somehow, however sad it made her feel, she made allowances, putting up with it, knowing that she shouldn't. That son of hers had filled her with an ineffable love of rapturous intensity, an exquisite elation beyond her wildest dreams. Truly sublime. She had been blown away by the thrilling, beautiful feeling, the nearest thing to transcending into heaven. At the time none of her other children had made her feel quite so special inside. Where had it all gone wrong? As a family they were tight-knit and loyal. None of them would let him down, but he treated them all the same, like shit. Quite honestly she was sick of smoothing things over. She understood that having lived away for at least five years, he had no desire to return and adjusting was going to take time.

The 'use-by date' on the milk had expired. This called for

a very substantial baked rice pudding. She buttered the sides of a no longer white enamel dish with a blue rim, favoured by celebrity chefs to show off their authentic recipes and into it added the rice, some of which stuck to the buttery grease, a little sugar, a knob of butter, the milk and a peppering of nutmeg. The long slow cooking softened and swelled the tight white grains, eventually absorbing the generous quart of milk. All afternoon a frosted mesh of condensation clung to the windows. Where it accumulated and gravity could hold it no longer, a bead of water slowly rolled down the window, unravelling daylight, like a puckered ribbon. She had acquired the dish in a Rotary Club Auction a long time ago. It had been in a cardboard box, along with all manner of odds and ends. It was lot 32. Going to the auction had become an event to look out for in February. Held in the hall next to the United Reform Church she and her children would preview before lunch to decide on what to bid for, then return for the auction at 2 p.m. The electrical goods like radiograms were on the stage, bulky goods like wardrobes and bookcases stood around the sides, covered in boxes of bric-a-brac. Heavy mowers, deck chairs and bikes cluttered round the entrance. A hush fell as people took their seats and the auctioneer started the proceedings. Hands and nods indicated interest to the auctioneer. It was pure entertainment. Laughter broke out and crescendos of 'oohs' and 'aahs' rippled round the hall as people's bids were successful or not. After a while, tea was served and everyone milled around talking about their good or bad fortune. The most covetous items were kept to the end, as was paying. At home, discovering what had been bought was just as much fun and since then the white enamel dish had been the perfect container for baked rice pudding and a lot of other things besides.

'The time has come the walrus said, to talk of many things, of shoes and ships and ceiling wax and cabbages and kings.' But she didn't. Instead she said.
"How can you be so nice?"
"I'm always nice."

"You're not always nice. Sometimes you are horrible."
"That's outside interference."

At the beginning of the year a violent surging wave swept through her. Full of hope and expectation, she had an overwhelming feeling that something explosive was going to happen. Eager for the next day, then the next and the day after her exuberance overflowed. Soaring out of control she was light headed and buoyant at the possibility of something exciting happening, fuelling and feeding her insatiable appetite through the drab winter days. Exhilarated, the frantic dancing in her head didn't stop. Anything was possible. Not knowing which direction the fire would take, the flames licked, fanning out, curling and sparking. She was compulsive and alert to any opportunity, dizzy with anticipation, posting letters and sending emails. After a while the feeling subsided. Realizing that nothing was going to happen, the fire settled and she got on with the rest of the year.

Submitting her second manuscript to the publishers was pending. Checking the requirements on-line, she needed a letter, a synopsis and three chapters. Altogether there were twelve chapters, but had not called them anything until now. The manuscript had been ready to send for a couple of months and completed for over a year. It was finally ready. Also, it had been six months since contacting three radio programmes about her published book. It was time to remind them and she wrote again. No news was good news and no news was not good news.

Then something did happen and how proud she was, seeing her son's name brought to the attention of the art world. It had first come to light in the autumn, having been selected from a host of international artists by Charlotte Bonham-Carter from Charles Saatchi's Online Gallery. From the promising write-up *Swell*, constructed of latex and steel had been chosen for a prestigious show in Detroit and taken out of storage and sent across the water. Chasing rainbows.

Its pure ringing brightness cut the dark into slices. Like a polished blazer button, the cool steel moon gleamed. Suspended, it presided over the sprinkling of twinkling stars flung across the sky. It left a mat of light on the landing. Slowly the mat got thinner. By morning it had gone.

When it could stay there no longer it fell out of the leaden sky, silently spiralling down and down to land on the ice-cold ground. She was afraid of the snow, afraid of its innocence since that January day a long time ago. The reason for her journey on that day was that she had taken a job more than thirty miles from home. Her youth and energy and the incentive of the luring increase in salary had to be worth the travelling. It had snowed in the night. Not impassable. She never forgot. Dirty ruts of cruel frosty slush had formed where heavy traffic had pressed into the snow. A dustbin lorry on the approaching slip-road barged in to join the cautious queue. But that meant that there was no room for her. She remembered the oncoming yellow Escort. Then nothing. Next, she was hanging upside down in her seatbelt and the couple from the yellow Escort standing beside her car, ready with a fire extinguisher. Whenever snow fell, she remembered. She was happy enough to walk in the snow, play in the snow and look at the snow. Driving in it however, made her feel physically sick. Never one to be late she was out first thing ensuring her car was completely free of the moiré of frost, spraying and scraping the windows inside and out. Wedged firmly in her seatbelt she was rigid with fear, her hands locked like a vice around the steering wheel, barely out of third gear all the way to work, no acceleration, no braking, no radio, no music, total concentration. Instead of reversing as she always did into her parking place, she cautiously edged in forwards, thankful to have arrived unscathed. Relieved to be getting out of the car, her legs turned to jelly and her heart pounded, her boots pressed into the snow.

Like a double head of steam their breath panted into the sub-zero air. She and her husband walked as one, slipping and sliding, concentrating on every step. Hunched and wrapped against the stabbing cold, their gloved hands clasped, gripping tighter when one or other slipped on the glassy surface, they took themselves off to the corner shop a mile away to get the aptly named 'Crap Chat', a weekly magazine full of crap, that her husband insisted buying because it gave the man in the Cadbury shop some trade. With barely room to turn round, it was stuffed from floor to ceiling with every conceivable convenience. Replacing his gloves, he tucked the magazine under his arm and finding her hand, they retraced their footprints left firmly in the snow. Arriving home again, their faces glowed and their bodies throbbed.

Poem for Haiti

For the earth that shivered its skin like an old horse
For the shout of the sun, of the earth as it broke its heart
For the white palace that fell into itself like snow
For the hospital, for its rows of white graves
For the cathedral that folded on emptiness
calling God's name as it went
For its psalms of sorrow, the prayers of the living and dead
For each house crushed with its cots and cushions and cups
cooking pots pressed between pages of stone
For the small lung of air that kept someone alive
For the rescuer's hand reaching into the void
For the slip of a life from its grip
For the smile of daylight on a woman's face
For her daughter dead in the dark
For the baby born in the rubble
For tomorrow's whistling workmen
with their hods of bricks
For scaffolding and walls rising from the grave
over rosaries of bones

By Gillian Clarke, National Poet of Wales
January 2010

Unexpectedly, she went to London, primarily to deliver her son's suit, needed for the following weekend. Absorbed in her book, the effortless journey slipped past. The sky reached down and touched the earth shrouding it in a damp cold mist. It was a year since publication and apart from proof reading, which she had to say she didn't do well because she tended to rush, she hadn't read it since writing it several years ago. Knowing the story so well, she read quickly and turned pages rapidly. Re-reading the familiar words she found three mistakes, glaring errors, but easy to miss when there is something to say that needs to be written there and then, in case it is crowded out by the moment. Casting a critical eye the mistakes were small, a coma instead of a full stop, followed by a new sentence. Bravely written and economically written, there were no wasted words, padding it out, increasing the word count. Both her children had found the first page unbearably sad and got no further, but were sick of people asking them about it and didn't know, and it was their intention to read it. The first page made her sad too. "It is sad." She said, proceeding to tell them about the phone call home, desperately pushing euros into the slot, aching to hear a familiar voice. Barely able to speak, but trying. The firm hard drone, when the money ran out and she hadn't finished and she hadn't said goodbye. Her son returning the receiver and saying later that mum had phoned and that she was having a nice time. The back door open, crumbs and a jammy knife on the bread-board. Waiting for her son outside Clapham Station the flower stall was setting up. Nimble fingers carefully transferred fresh flowers from their protective cardboard boxes to buckets of water. Cleverly arranged to capture and entice an impetuous sale. Gulping down the intoxicating smell she breathed deeply. She needed all her strength to avoid an irrational purchase. Her son came into view and she walked towards him. Together they went to the British Library to check that her published book was there. Really she wanted to see it on the shelf, but the ordering system only allowed her to see it in a reading room and that was going to take over an hour. Anyway, she didn't have the relevant documents to register. Checking on the computer had to suffice. The two of them met Alex at the usual place in Charlotte Street. They talked about the earthquake and religion and food and her books and flights to Detroit. The restaurant was not busy. It had been laid out differently and the décor had had undergone a subtle change. Along the long wall opposite, fathers sat facing their daughters, taking them for lunch, leaning in, their elbows on the table, talking and sharing. The girls were no age, early teens. Their fathers had missed them growing and playing. While they had been working, time had slipped past. The only way to make it right was to indulge and treat, to spare the racking guilt. Too soon, lunch time ended. Out in the cold again, her son took some pictures at arm's length of the three of them, they hugged on the corner and said goodbye. Knowing that they would be there, rubbing against the pressing throng until they dissolved into the crowd, she didn't turn round and wave but crossed the road to make her way back to Euston, not wanting to feel the fleeting disappointment of parting.

EMAILS

As proof of her unfolding story she had kept the early emails as a record. Not truly convinced about the virtual world, she printed out her brother's emails. Having them in print assured her that she was living and he was too and that she was not going mad, inventing stories and that finding him along with other brothers and sisters was real. Reading them again, the complicatedness of it all was difficult to fathom.

It was three of Donald's many cousins, on his mother's side, that were interested in family history, and made the first contact, initially acting as the go-between.

Dear Chris 11th July 2007
I am hoping that you will be able to help. It is a bit of a long story. My father Jonathan Weir had a son with Dorothy Lillian Verrall in August 1946, his name on his birth certificate is Donald Keith MacLaughlan Weir. I contacted the register office for Scotland and England and they did not get married. The son was born in Stirling. On the descendants of Verrall everything seems to match, dates etc. Dorothy Lillian was married to James Angus and came from the Brisbane area. Can I assume the Brisbane connection? Donald married Doreen Marion Mathias in November 1964 and they had three children, Colin born May 1965, Robert born October 1967 and Jacqueline born February 1975, but I don't know where. On the birth certificate, Dorothy Lillian listed her occupation as an insurance agent and her address as Cadden Lea, Thornhill Stirling. Dorothy Lillian was born in 1909 so by 1946 would have been 37, in those days that would have seemed old. There was only one child. Until the end of 1947 she lived in Stenhousemuir. But where did she go then, with her son? Or was he adopted? My father was with my mother in 1950 as I was born in 1951. I would dearly like to contact Donald and/or his children.

Louise

Hi Paul 11th July 2007
Hope you are all well, and not washed away. We are so cold down here. It's been windy also. I have forwarded this on to you, in a hope that you might have a clue as to something on this line. I have no more than I have on my file, I didn't even know she had been to Scotland. I wonder why. Please bring out the family skeletons. I have sent her what I had on Dorothy Lillian, which is not much.
Chris

G'day Chris (you old closet rattler you!) 12th July 2007
Yep, everyone is fine, still haven't got away yet, been too cold down your way and Canberra, might see if we can get away in the spring. Anyway, to business. Donald (Scotty) Weir is my cousin, I rang this morning but he is out and about today but spoke to his wife Margaret and will ring him tonight. Apparently he has no knowledge of any reli's on his father's side, he believed his father was killed in an accident in England just after the war. I will let you know more after I have spoken to him.
Paul

Hi Louise 13th July 2007
Here is an email forwarded on for Donald Weir – your half-brother!
Sue

Hello Sue 13th July 2007
I would be grateful if you would pass this on to Louise. Wow a half-sister and I always thought I was an only child. Yes, my mother and I came to Australia in September 1949. Mum was an Australian citizen so she had first preference on the ships coming here. The rest is a long and involved story so it may have to wait until we make direct contact.
Donald

Hello Louise 14th July 2007

Me, former wife and 3 kids. Jacqueline was born on 14th January. We previously had another child before getting married, adopted out and only found us in 1994, christened Jennifer Matthias born on 31/8/1963

Donald

Hello Louise 15th July 2007

I will look out all that I have left from Mum, boy what a conniving old bugger he was. Mum told me they went on a day trip then married in northern France in a small church in a small village because of the Church of England's requirements such as papers, posting of the bans etc. Any wonder Mum warned my first wife the Weirs are as randy as rabbits, she already knew this!

More photos and whatever I can find I will forward. As for coming to England, not now but maybe some time in the future.

Donald

Hello Louise 21st July 2007

If you could scan and email any photos that you have, I would appreciate it. A lot of Australians went to Britain back then as Aussies then were British citizens and didn't need a passport to travel there. Mum went to the 'Mother Country' I believe in 1934 to work as a governess and tour Europe. I remember various photos of Egypt, Spain, Italy and France. Her passport was very busy, just like a modern day backpacker. In 1937 she was working for the Black family in Birmingham (twin boys). This is where she met our father and set up house. Unfortunately there is very little left in the way of photos or paperwork. She went into a nursing home in 1984

Donald

Hi Louise 23rd July 2007

No the attachment didn't come through. Next time! It is a bit tricky until you get the hang of it. Unfortunately I have no idea why Dorothy Lillian went to Scotland. I guess Donald will have to dig around to find out why. Problem is, most of the old *ones are already long gone. I also don't know if she did marry James Pallet Angus. With a name like that you would think he was Scotch also. I don't know if Donald has a death certificate for her, but it would say if she was married. Sorry I'm not much help with this line, my husband is Donald's 3rd cousin so they come from different children, but have the same great, great grandfather. Seeing as Paul is into their line, he may be able to scout around and find out a bit about this line's descendants. I have Verralls from before them. Please tell me, who is K Langridge? And do her Verralls come from Lewes or Eastbourne?*

Chris

Hello Louise 24th July 2007

I take it Robert is your husband. Pity we didn't know about each other then as we could have met somewhere. Great Ocean Road has excellent scenery. I don't remember a marriage certificate but on her passport she was Weir, amended from Verrall presumably by the embassy. The wedding was supposedly just before the war. The ship we travelled to Aus on was the Arcadia. I have an aluminium drink coaster from it which I will photograph and enclose in the future. Sorry about the cricket, ha ha. You should have come to Brisbane, if you check the atlas, where we live is north of Brisbane near Bribie Island, middle of winter now and temp down to 9°C. Enclosed photos of my wife Margaret and myself with my motorcycle and me in a kilt at Christmas or New Year.

Donald

Hello Louise 25th July 2007

By the look of the square photo, corrugated iron etc, it could be Australia, but it is not me. Mum mentioned relis in New Zealand. Could there be more? My ears don't (didn't) stick out like that and I've never been allowed to have a short haircut like that. The other photo of the younger child with the chair could be me!

Donald

Hi Louise 25th July

Thanks, got it this time. I had a look at K Langridge's stuff and can assure you it is not correct. We had nothing to do with the toffee nosed Lewes Verralls, all ours were labourers from Eastbourne. Can send you if you want.

Chris

Dear Chris 25th July

I'm not doing family trees anyway. I could see that the Verralls were from the Sussex area. Are you in touch with your family there? Do you think that James Pallet Angus is wrong, listed as Dorothy Lillian's first husband?

Louise

Hi Louise 26th July 2007

As far as I know, Dorothy Lillian married the Angus guy later, have no info yet, but will see what I can find out. No, not in touch with any Verralls in Sussex, Our lot came in 1843, so didn't ever have contact.

Chris

Hello Louise 31st July 2007

Mum married James Angus in 1975, I think ???? I'll look it up. It could be a wedding photo, I don't know ??? I was told my name MacLaughlan was traditionally given to the first born son ?????? Don't feud, it's a waste of time and energy! Tell Chris to contact me if she want to, my mobile is almost always on and the home phone is cheaper. A spin on the bike will be arranged, I've had a bike of some sort or other since I turned 14 and haven't gone without one for more than six months. It's like a drug. A recent photo of you would be appreciated and it looks like you can use a scanner with the best of us. Don't be shy !!!!!!

Donald

Hello Louise 3rd August 2007

Mum married James Angus on 21st Dec 1968. The other photo is Aunt Jean and Sonny's wedding, can't read the back of the photo properly. Too much vino with supper. The writing on the copy of my birth cert. is Mum's. I had to get another when I applied for a passport in 1994 as I laminated the one I had to stop it deteriorating further and it was not acceptable.
Donald

Hello Donald 19th August 2007

Thank you for answering my questions. I was away last week for a few days and on Sunday I am going away for two weeks so you will not hear from me for a while, then, I will be back to school. I will call when I'm back.
Louise

Hello Louise 19th August 2007

So what do you do for a living? Still waiting for the photo of you and Robert. The photo of you in the mortar-board and gown with the orange sash is for what? Gee I don't know what to do, I've never had a sister or two before !!!
Donald

Hello Louise 5th September 2007

I'm glad someone in our family went to college. My education stalled at 13 (the end of 8th grade, even though I passed the Scholarship exam with a 93.5% pass) much to the disgust of Mum. I discovered in the following order, I think, Motorcycles, Alcohol and Women (Girls actually) although they have always been older than me ??? I started a mechanic apprenticeship but when Doreen became pregnant I left to get a better paying job (responsible person). I started in tyre servicing and have pretty well stayed doing that all my life, going from car to giant earthmover tyres. I have driven trucks, buses and articulated vehicles. I got interested in safety during my working life in the coalmines and did some courses. (Trainer and Assessor, Workplace Health and Safety Officer, Rehabilitation Coordinator, First Aid etc) I left Brisbane in

1978 after a rather messy divorce to go to the coalmines in Central Queensland and stayed there for over 20 years. Meeting Margaret in 1977 was the catalyst for me to leave. We were married on 17/01/1987 and have been together since. We see Margaret's children more than mine as two of them still blame Margaret for the divorce.

Donald

Hello Louise 17th September 2007

No I don't have enough to occupy myself with but hopefully that will change from 22nd October when I start a new job. Probably around 60-70 hours per week with around 1 hour travelling each way.

Mum's signature never changed much from then until her remarriage, a little shakier but very much the same. I haven't got to Mum's wedding certificate to James Angus yet.

Good to see I had something in common with the old bugger, with my first child born in an unmarried mother's home at least your mum kept you with her, not like my first wife and myself.

I had heard Mum mention Stenhousemuir but I don't remember in what context. I can recall Mum talking about Prudential Insurance?????

I smoked from when I was 12yrs until I was 38 then I decided it was a waste of my health and money (Scottish heritage???). I still like a drink on a warm day.

I've worn glasses since I was in my mid 20s and my hair is due to the Verrall's side of the family. All Mum's brothers that I knew had a head full of hair until they died.

I hope these little snippets of information all help the big picture.

I will need an address to post Christmas cards etc or if I decide to sneak over to England. Can I get you to take my savings book to the bank and get it updated? If there are sufficient funds I may be able to afford to come to England. Ha Ha.

What tartan is "our" Father's kilt? Am I allowed to wear that tartan according to the custom? Is the sporran still with it and is it in good condition?

Does Fiona have an email address and is she as interested in all this as you are?

All these questions ???????????????????????????????? and more.

Donald

Hello Donald, 17th September 2007

I'm glad to hear that you start work again, long hours though!!!

Yes, my mum kept me, although she was encouraged to give me up for adoption. If you look on The Haven, Yateley, you will see where I was born, I keep meaning to get the book.

The snippets are good.

Do let me know if you are going to sneak over to England and no I do not think you will have sufficient funds in the savings book.

The tartan of the kilt in the trunk is The Black Watch of The Argyle and Southerland Highlanders. But both Fiona and I when we were young wore the Ancient Baird, which is 'our' grandmother's maiden name. From what I remember, the sporran malts a bit.

I do not know Fiona's email address but Jean, Walter's wife who lives in Denny would like to contact you. I do not think that she uses a computer. Do let me know if I can forward your address, otherwise I will say nothing. She knows that I have found you. Walter is the youngest of the first Weir family, born in 1932. Walter is poorly.

Louise

Hello Louise, 19th September 2007

Please feel free to forward on my address to Jean as I would love to hear from her. Give it to anyone and everyone you see fit to. I would love to have both the kilt and the sporran if you don't want them or your children don't. At 75 Walter is entitled to feel a little poorly. All I need to do is win Lotto and I'll be right over. Of course I'll let you know when I'm coming

to England. Have you been watching the 20-20 cricket? Australia isn't invincible!!!
Donald

Hello Louise 5th October 2007
A short email to show you the collar jewellery which was on our father's uniform. I have had it since I was a teenager but I couldn't find them until today. The thistle was with them and the diamond shaped button has the thing on the back broken.
Donald

Dear Donald, 14th November 2007
How are things?
I've been looking back over your messages. You said that you could see that your mum's name had changed from Verrall to Weir on her passport. Will you photocopy it and send it? I'm going to see if I can find out if they were married.

If they went on a day trip to France I will start with Boulogne and Calais and immediate villages. My French is zilch but I'm going to have a go. I've got a feeling that they were married. Your mother would not have seen any reason why they should not marry. You have got his name and your mum was with him until she left and they were together for some years before you were born. It just doesn't add up. What do you think when you really think about it. Surely in those days your mum would expect to marry. What would her family have thought? I'm just so curious. I also want to know who the little boy is with the sticking out ears. I might check out where 'Dad' was around the beginning of the fifties, where we used to live.

Let me know if you come across anything that is interesting. Also, can I forward the bank book?
Louise

Hello Louise 15th November 2007

I don't have the passport but I can remember as a kid looking at it. Maybe the boy with the sticking out ears in the photo is one of the older boys?????? Maybe ask Walter or one of the others. Feel free to forward the bank book and thank you.

Donald

Dear Donald 26th November 2007

Have collected the bankbooks together along with the paperwork. It seems funny sending them to you. A year ago when I started to find out where you were I hoped that they would lead me to you. They will be posted on Tuesday. But no, the photo is not one of the Denny children. I have asked, but anyway the clothes are wrong for their young years. No, I'm sure it is a child brought up at the same time as me.

I have to say, there is no love lost between 'our' father and me.

Louise

Dear Louise 26th November 2007

I'm so glad you finally found me but there are now so many more questions. Pity about you not getting along with the old man. At least you knew him, for better or worse, which is more than I did. As a child at time I envied all the kids with siblings and two parents but maybe a session with a shrink might have helped ????? oops waaaay too late.

Donald

Dear Louise 27th November 2007

Remember when I left the area I was only three years old so I have no or very little memory of where I lived or of 'Father'. I thought of going to Britain and looking up relatives when I retire and that is still on the agenda. My Mum told me he was dead (and maybe he was to her), a three year old believes and trusts his Mum, it's only as you get much older do you get cynical and less trusting of your elders (and now I'm one of them).

Yes it was that bad not having a Father, getting teased at school and no male figure to look up to and to be a guide and mentor. Yes, she was a very strong person and I was alone for a lot of my life as she went to work, leaving home at 5.30am and returning home at about 7.30pm. I learned to cook and look after myself from an early age. I was always told he was dead.

Donald

Hello Louise 2nd January 2008

Sorry to be so slack in replying to your emails. Yes I have received the bank books and your Christmas card two days apart and will bring the bank book back to Britain with me when I come over. Yes Margaret and I have both read your book, what can I say, what a rotten thing the old bugger was. I'm almost glad I didn't know him. Margaret said much the same, only worse. I do hope writing the book has been a bit therapeutic for you and got some of the hurt and loathing off your chest. Margaret says she feels for you. The weather in Melbourne has been terrific but here in Brisbane it has been awful, rain daily then hot and steamy, 30c and up to 90% humidity. My Aunt Jean, the last of Mum's siblings died on Christmas Day and was buried on the 28th and believe it or not, she had a photo of me, sent to her of me in 1947, it is attached. Written on the back in Mum's handwriting is, Donald, John and I will be coming home as soon as John gets demobbed and we can get passage to Australia, Love Dorrie. I have asked Cousin Lynne if I can have it. I scanned it at her place in the album. It was stuck down and the writing was difficult to read. As you can see, someone has already bent it around trying to read the back.

Donald.

It truly did suggest that her father and Donald's mother were a family.

The day, well hardly a day, started at 1p.m. when she finally had time to herself, the first for months. With the persistent noise and constant clamouring, there was a need to get off the treadmill, a need for silence. Firstly, she sat at the computer, not especially doing much, more preoccupied with staring out of the window at the cold dank greyness hanging over the field beyond, people walking their dogs, tense and hunched. There was an email from Jean. Agnes, Jean's sister-in-law and her half-sister had died. The phone rang pulling her away from Scotland, distracting her train of thought. She missed the call, but knowing it to be her husband, she called back and once in the kitchen again organised an onion on the wooden board, peeled and cut in half along with three cloves of garlic, crushed and a stick of celery diced. She walked into town, for fresh air as much as anything and to collect a prescription and to check the charity shops for bargains. There were none. Returning home, she reheated the coffee and took the remains of the biscotti from the full-English breakfast earlier and her book and read until a drowsy aura prompted the removal of her glasses and her hair band, both of which dug into her scalp. She didn't sleep, but dozed on and off disturbed by the grating sound of an electric saw being used intermittently further down the road. By four, she was in the kitchen again. Her son phoned. It was the pre-view evening at the Museum Of New Art in Detroit and understandably he was excited, and rightly so, truly an achievement. Sitting in the kitchen, she once again picked up her book, devouring the pages with one eye on the dinner. The rock hard chair was softened with a worn, wafer thin cushion. The fabric was a deep Santorini blue and the embroidered fish were losing their fins. She remembered buying the cushion cover in the heat of the evening, finding it difficult to choose one from the hundreds piled high in a shop in Sharm el Sheik. They were made completely by hand, dextrous clever hands stitching the pictures in dusty outlying villages in the ochre coloured desert. The phone rang. There was a hold-up. She turned down the heat under the paella. Further phone calls followed. She turned the heat off and sat down again to read.

As the crowded train approached Wembley, the passengers

became restless. Young and old turned to look at the saintly arc of flashing steel reaching into the rain-splattered sky. Necks craned to see. Children's faces pressed against the glass. "Look mummy, there's Wembley." Men nudged each other. "There's Wembley." They said in their soft old voices. Murmuring, they paid homage to their heroes and the hallowed turf, remembering the year when it was England's turn to win the world cup. The date fixed in their memories, remembered like the Battle of Hastings or the signing of the Magna Carta or The Great War or the Second World War. Recently rebuilt on the old site, the new stadium looked out of place in the worn out neighbourhood of North London, much of which was shabby and neglected. Within moments it had passed. She had been to Wembley several times with her son to the drum centre buried deep in a swathe of industrial tract Her son, there to buy his first drum kit saved for by doing months and months of washing up before the days of the dishwasher. Alighting at the station they crossed the road and made their way down the steps to the big wide concourse that led to the famous white towers, so fondly remembered. So many could only dream of being there. It was wasted on her.

At least ten lined the desk in their corporate identity clothing, like holiday reps or an airline crew. Along the mile high wall behind them were etched the company names of those who rented office space. Her publisher was not amongst them. Tentatively she leaned onto the desk and enquired. Their office was situated on the thirtieth floor. Happy to know that it was, she didn't need escorting to it. It was raining and it was cold so she made for the shops deep underground, beneath the urban spill of gleaming steel and glass and tons of concrete used to construct the invading towers that reached into the dreary February sky. She had been before to Canary Wharf on just such a mission, but had been disappointed when not to be able to travel on the DLR, because of engineering maintenance on the line and instead had to make the journey on a replacement bus service. It wasn't the same. It had been a Saturday and ghostly quiet, seeing only a security guard standing with his feet astride, hands behind his back, looking through the plate glass onto what he saw every day or turning and passing the time of day with the receptionist, busy filing her nails, waiting for the shift to end. This time it was the raw wet day that caused the absence of people. Occasionally someone crossed at the lights, but below ground it was heaving. Not one to eat on the move, she installed herself on a high stool opposite HMV having some lunch, people watching, the ultimate spectator-sport. Some would not know what the initials HMV stood for, like her when she saw AKA. She thought it was an African name until she noticed that it appeared too often on the register. However she did know what HMV stood for and remembered clearly the music shop in Wellington Street in Luton where there were booths to listen to the latest vinyl sounds, when Luton thrived and jived, before re-generation and pedestrianisation, and block paving covered over the problems. Like an artery George Street had allowed the town to breath, bringing in traffic and people and prosperity. Now, run-down and neglected it is left to its own devices. Left to hooded figures lurking in doorways, people with time on their hands and women, veiled and scurrying into the shadows. Like bad teeth the shabby boarded-up shops line the main street and the traffic skirts the town centre altogether, leaving crime and vandalism to feast on the rotting half eaten core out of sight. It was grim and so opposite to the indulgence of Canary Wharf. Out of the over warm carpeted offices above, the never-ending human traffic streamed past, in suits and shirt-sleeves, high heels and long legs. Like working ants, people scurried this way and that in the glitzy malls and walkways, on their own or sometimes in twos, shopping and eating and running out of time and collecting dry cleaning and carrying morsels in little brown carrier bags. Like addicts desperate for their next fix, nimble fingers urgently flicked open their miniscule screens to check their messages or type a text or talk rapidly on phones pressed close to their ears, as if life itself depended on it. She felt like a visitor, an intruder in a world she knew nothing about and even though she window-shopped in the very same shops elsewhere, somehow they were different. Although she had felt fine about herself when leaving home she no longer did, instead she felt clumsy and old. The people here thought about their appearance, they took risks and made decisions and they were in a rush. Surfacing later into the pouring rain at Green Park station, she crossed the road to buy a colourful stripy umbrella. Never had she experienced such persistent rain when shopping. Feeling better away from the unfamiliar, she caught the bus and made her way towards Knightsbridge. With renewed energy she checked her favourite shops and like the previous day at Tring museum, the 'naughty noughties' children were out in force, in tow, harassed mothers, enduring half term holidays, putting up with their children's moans and groans. At the museum many children had been running about, not the least interested in the animals exhibited. One mother let rip. "Shut the fuck up." Silence descended in the gallery. Shocked, the humans stopped in their tracks and the animals stared blindly from their glass cages as they had for a hundred years. They had seen the humans before. They had seen their brutality.

She and her husband had spent the weekend with her sister and husband. Their latest project was to convert a fairly modest bungalow into a house. They revelled in the mess and the cost and the tears and the aching backs. Martin, her sister's husband, usually went along with her plans for a quiet life. His wife was the driving force. Before moving away she would see her sister often, but over the years, as the children had grown up and their own 'new' careers had taken hold there seemed less time and less reason to get together. Until four years ago, her sister would return to visit their mother when the racking guilt got too much. But when their mother died, visits lessened and now she would see her only once or twice a year. Whenever she did she felt dissatisfied. It was a pockmarked relationship. Undoubtedly there was bond between them but whither it was love, she didn't know. In her presence, she felt belittled. Her sister had charisma and was smarter and cleverer. She spoke eloquently, with conviction, fluently and confidently. Making use of expensive words she had the art of stringing them together in a convincing way, so compelling that even boring things became interesting. The ebb and flow of her voice lingered long after she had stopped talking. She was always advising and making suggestions. Have you seen? Or have you read? Or have you tried? Well no, she hadn't. Her sister was well informed, remembering names of people in films and titles of songs and who sang them, knowing every ailment in Latin and every medicinal cure to put it right. She too found time to sing and she painted vast canvases. Her skeletal frame was effortlessly thin and looked cool hung in someone else's cast-offs, rummaged for in her local charity shop. She on the other hand seemed to have nothing interesting to say, or if she did she was crowded out and her voice was lost. She was no match. Her sister always won and got her own way. There was no compromise. Their mother used to confide in her that she was hard, like her father. At the time she went along with what her mother said, not really understanding but wanting to please, vying for her mother's attention. Now that she was older, she could see what she meant.

There never seemed to be time to say what she wanted to say. Her mind was charged. She wanted to tell her sister about her years of crushing resentment, her destructive envy and her insane jealousy, but she became tongue tied, strangled by her own words, unable to speak. She wanted to feel the closeness that her sister had found with her 'new' friends, she wanted the intimacy of sitting round the table, or walking against the wind, arms linked. She had adopted a new way of life, a life that would never be hers. She didn't fit. To her, their short time together often seemed superficial, their lives shallow. They skirted around things. In thirty years they had drifted apart, gone their separate ways, their mother and their own children keeping them together, but now, they too had gone and only fleetingly spoken of. She seemed to evade the nitty-gritty, only saying what she wanted you to hear, preferring to remain uplifted as though everything was sweetness and light. A snapshot. If her sister stayed overnight, she worried constantly, wanting to please, lighting the fire, eating the right food, including oats and fresh fruit and water, not too much fat, throw in some super-foods. She would even think about her clothes and what she looked best in and be embarrassed by her husband's slovenly appearance. God it was endless. To her sister, impressions were everything. She seemed to aspire to the glossy magazine on the coffee table look. She had changed.

Much progress had been made in the house and they sat having supper, her sister called dinner, supper, in their newly finished kitchen. There were no napkins to dab or to protect laps from food that had a mind of its own and slip off the fork. "You need some napkins." She said, tempted to get some kitchen roll from the dispenser.

"Yes, but they need ironing." She retorted.

"You don't have to iron them. They can be stressed and crumpled. I will buy some when I am shopping."

Sloane Street was somewhat quieter and still there was no sign of spring in the gardens. Peter Jones was such a satisfying shop, it was tasteful and affordable and the assistants assisted. Walking through the china department she could see tablecloths and napkins banked up in a wave of colour in the corner. Her sister had wanted white, but doubted her laundering prowess. It fell short as did her ironing skills. Maintaining white would be a chore, so she settled for blue and delegated her husband to iron them. There, displayed on a wooden rack were the perfect hemstitched napkins in cornflower blue, neatly folded into triangles, exactly what she wanted. Feeling pleased, she bought four. It would be a start. In the pouring rain she met up with her sons at the Chelsea Potter, then went on for some food further down the road in the rustic charm of 'Made in Italy'. She didn't like to think that it was part of a chain or a group, but more bespoke.

Twelve hours earlier queues had threaded their way from the four manned counters and the numerous ticket machines cluttering the concourse. It had been heaving with people. Now, apart from the two policemen leaning at the door, it was desolate. Despite the pressure to have a mobile phone, she had never been tempted or persuaded and while she could appreciate their hand-held desire and didn't doubt their appeal, she could live without one. People had become dependent on them, even pupils at school ambled about with their eyes fixed on the screen, attached to wires that they tried to hide in their hair or inside their collar, or held the device in the palm of one hand while the index finger of the other stroked the screen. They didn't see the scudding sky beyond the apex of glass, or marvel at the construction that was their school. There was no way she could be tempted. As she crossed to speak to the policemen her loyal and dependable husband had seen her silhouetted against the brightness of the station. He flashed the car headlights. The crowded day brought no sleep.

True to her word, the following afternoon, she posted the napkins with love.

She had an email from 'Woman's Hour' saying that her book had not been brought to their attention and that they did not review books anyway. Replying, she said that she realised they did not review books but that the content was so appropriate for their programme. Having a reply was good, as was a letter from the publisher saying that her second book was with the editors and to be patient. Something amazing was going to happen. A month later it did. The letter lay on the mat. She could see from the postmark, as she pushed open the door, laden with bags, that it was from the publisher. Immediately dumping the bags, she picked it up and opened it. Removing the letter her eyes read as she unfolded it. The Chief Editor had requested to view the whole manuscript. The frantic music in her head started up again. The euphoria returned. At the same time she contacted the local radio station, the one that crashed into her car every fifteen minutes, intruding and invading her space. Yes, they were interested in doing something and wanted to know if she would participate in a feature called Book Battle, where two local authors flag-up their books, encouraging the listeners to read them.

Surely it couldn't get much worse. 740,591 in Amazon books sales rank. She wrote a review. Be the first. It seemed odd to her to be conceited enough to write one. It did get worse, 743,309 and even worse. Then for no apparent reason it would be ranked 224,357. Now how could that be? Did sales suddenly improve? Unable to resist, she checked most days, knowing that she shouldn't, like people who watched their weight, stepping on the scales every time they walked past. In the beginning she regularly bought all the daily papers to check the reviews, hoping to find her novel listed in the top ten paperbacks and just in case she had missed something she also scrolled through their websites. Gradually she weaned herself off the desire to check. How did she think that there was the remotest chance of being reviewed?

The bitter cost of clothes, nice clothes, made her think that she ought to resurrect the sewing machine. And so she sat in the sunny square at the kitchen table restoring the fraying edges of an old skirt, cropped a year ago for a fresh look and left hanging in limbo in the wardrobe with its matching jacket.

After the whiteness of snow, the grass looked brightly green, the sort of glaring shocking green that fashion designers favoured to create a daring impact, yet impossible to wear unless you were a leprechaun or Keira Knightley in *Atonement*. Stunted from the months of frost, the grass was manicured neatly within the paths. Surely winter was turning the corner, it had gone on for too long and outstayed its welcome. Even the children were no longer excited by the persistent flurries. Flooding followed. The waterlogged ground squelched. Swans and ducks swam in the fields. Water lapped at gravestones. Lead grey skies insisted.

The pale yellow sun was there but it had no shape. Its thin light dissolved behind the high cloud, was wasted, like spilt milk.

"That's the end of the loaf."
"No, it's not."
She was not one to lie. Officially it was the end of the loaf, but she had skimmed off the meanest amount and presented it

toasted, spread thinly with butter and jam and cut diagonally. He turned the triangle over to show her.

"I thought you said it was not the end of the loaf."

Checking through the manuscript before posting she needed to make sure there were no inaccuracies and needed her husband to confirm some dates. Not that the actual dates were mentioned, but she needed to know so that her chapters could be defined. Her husband reached into the drawer below the television for his 2008 diary. Written down, were all the key events and happenings of the year. There was an opportunity and it seemed appropriate, so she said,

"What do you mean by outside interference?" She knew that he wouldn't come across it in the diary, even though he still held it idly, flicking through the small fluttery pages, stopping here and there to recapture a moment or compare the weather.

"What do you mean?" he said.

"Oh you know, you said it a while back and I wondered what you meant." A wall of silence descended. He had no idea what she was talking about or he chose not to know. Either way, letting the dust settle, she closed the lid on her thoughts. Like other things it would still be there, eventually finding its way to the back of the drawer, along with the pieces of Lego and safety pins attached to dry cleaning labels and stamps, un-franked, prised carefully from envelopes with the intention of reusing and puffy packets, too good to throw away that she planned to use again, but never did.

The days were stretching out. In milder winters the hawthorn appeared earlier but this year spring was biding its time in the hedgerows. However, the promise of warmer days was uplifting and her husband began to shrug off his gloomy winter cloak. The tight brown twigs, swollen with leaf were waiting and when they could wait no longer their buds burst, their soft waxy shoots exploded, urgently flushing through the tangle of bare branches, tinting the hedge khaki. Within days the nibs of green ignited and the shoots uncurled, setting fire to the hedges. A wave of green washed around fields interspersed with frothy clouds of blackthorn. Keeping the audience waiting in the wings of March, the leaves on the trees did not rush onto the stage. Their entrance was slow and provocative and took several weeks, tempting, opening up a little more and a little more each day until a blur of steamy green gauze settled lightly on the framework of branches. Their showy optimism filled the air and she knew that for six months at least her husband would be all fired-up. By mid-May the trees were fabulous.

"It's the sort of day to strip the wallpaper in the sitting room." He said. And so it was on that cold March day that their friendship returned, sharing the lifting, sharing the carrying, working out between them how to get the settee through the door. An hour later, the room was empty. Deciding on a colour scheme was never going to be agreeable but after several papers were taped to the wall, they compromised. It had been twenty years since the room had been decorated and it undoubtedly needed attention. Having experimented with hanging wallpaper before, she failed to see what all the fuss was about. The paper was like a roll of cloth and needed to be cut to match and fit the room, like a body. Boldly she said that she didn't want to help if he was going to shout at her, not really thinking that she would be participating anyway, as she never had before. They tended to keep to their own jobs, she painted the ceiling and he painted the woodwork. This time she thought wrong. He wanted her to help and he needed her help. Together they mixed the wallpaper paste, she stirred while he filed the granules slowly into the bowl of water. From the back of the drawer she remembered being blamed for lumpy paste because she hadn't stirred fast enough. It was where her assistance had stopped. This time they unrolled each length of paper together, her husband climbed on the chair and marked the paper at the ceiling then passed her the pencil for her to mark it at the skirting board, between them, they carefully transferred the paper to the pasting table where it was trimmed and liberally applied with paste, then even more carefully returned to the wall to be matched and hung, brushed and smoothed, then trimmed at the top and bottom. This was how it happened until the whole room was done, in perfect harmony. She did not feel stressed or threatened or upset and he didn't swear or throw the tools down in a temper. Her only concern was that each roll of paper was from a different batch. She knew that she was flirting with trouble, but had been so tempted by the massive reduction in the price per roll. Through the shiny film wrapper they had all looked the same, but she knew that it was wrong. Her husband would know immediately if there was any change in the pattern or the colour or the texture. The shop assistant suggested that she removed the labels and not to tell him about the odd batch numbers. No-wonder people divorce, she thought. To blatantly cover-up the truth seemed even more dishonest. She was not comfortable deceiving her husband and it was not until the last length was hung without any obvious discrepancies that she breathed a sigh of relief. Had she been found out, the consequences would have been grim and her wallpapering days numbered. As it was, from her inherent thriftiness she had a lovely 'new' room with enough change for a lovely 'new' dress.

A letter arrived. Her manuscript was with the chief editor. Once again she continued to wait patiently. Meanwhile, she sent her book to a new TV book programme and *The Lady*, a weekly magazine that had dramatically changed its image. Heavy with embarrassment, she had simply missed her chance on 'Book Battle' and wasted an opportunity. Nerves and her self-consciousness had got the better of her and on air there was no vibrancy in her voice, it was dry and crumpled like a pile of dead leaves. Everything that she had planned to say drained away along with the two thirds of her body that soaked into her clothes leaving the third that was left feeling like a dried fish. There was nothing bright and vital to say and she repeated herself unnecessarily with not even a mention of where her book was set, which was a key point. She sighed. It was done. It couldn't be changed. After the darkness of the studio, she was relieved to be outside again. Slices of sunlight fell between the buildings and sharp black shadows were stamped upon the pavements. The experience had left her feeling bereft. Disappointed, she made her way back to the car, parked on the top level in the multi-story car park. Before leaving the car park, she had made sure what to do with the yellow counter that the machine had dispensed as she had entered. Why was it that every car park meter and swimming pool locker arrangement was different? In her mind she was angry with herself, angry that she had not done better. For God's sake she could talk. She talked all day long. "You sounded nervous." Said her friend on Monday morning. That was an understatement. Most days when she passed the BBC Three Counties 'Early Morning' radio offices on the way to work, she was reminded of that awful five minute episode. Her mind had been too congested. What she should have said was "Good afternoon, I am here today to convince you that my story *Patchwork* is well worth reading because ... " It would haunt her forever.

Still there were tremors. A lovely day out at the Oval spoilt because she refused to wind down her window and adjust her wing mirror. It was dark and she no longer liked driving in the dark. Besides the hallucinations of the dark, she had apparitions and phantom shadows to contend with and dangerous gaping potholes to negotiate, the legacy of months of icy conditions that had still not had their cavities filled with a plaster of asphalt and on top of that, her husband's criticism. No, she would not be swayed and kept both hands firmly on the wheel. How it annoyed him. Like it did when they returned home from a sunny walk and her car was parked in the wrong place, or hearing him cursing under his breath when she had forgotten to reposition the seat after driving his car. He liked his car parked where he wanted it, exactly as he left it, ready. Only the other day he was angered when she didn't call 1471 to find out who had just phoned, aware within a second that it was best to do so she picked up the receiver and dialled. Realizing when they were about to go out for a walk that she had no need for her reading glasses and wanted them back in the house and to pick up her sunglasses instead. From nowhere anger surged, everything about him altered, his grimace was enough to turn milk sour. Not daring to fetch the sun-glasses from the kitchen, only ten strides away, she went without. He asked later why she didn't enjoy the walk. The queasy uncertainty of the fractious undercurrent was un-nerving. With her senses keen, she was mindful and alert to the impatience in his voice.

Her son phoned. He was going to London and did she want to go. Well of course she wanted to go. And so he collected her at 7 a.m. the next morning. All the way they chatted about this and that and on reaching Brent Cross she was reminded of when she used to work in East Barnet and how she had to catch the bus home on the duel carriageway, telling her son how horrible it was being a pedestrian in the maze of concrete, the deafening noise, not noticed in a car and the dirt blowing about and underfoot and how, when she had time to spare in that hot summer term, she would pass her time cooling off in the chilled area of Marks and Spencer looking at the desserts and sometimes even buying one, to eat once seated on the bus, before she fell asleep. And how, as they drove down Finchley Road, I say down because where her friend lived it was on the hill, her flat so large that the grand piano looked insignificant. How did they get it up to the fifth floor? They had to stop. In the midst of the rush hour everyone stopped to let them pass. Coming from the left were horses, fine, good tempered animals, their heads held high. The Household Cavalry. At least ten minutes passed while the cavalcade crossed the road. Swinging through the empty streets he dropped her off behind Harrods, where the seriously rich people lived. Arriving too early for shops to be open, she made her way along Knightsbridge and Sloane Street to Sloane Square and Kings Road, her favourite haunts, stopping every now and then to window shop. Later, she bought a dress and the all-important white cardigan that she had been craving for a while, in order to create a vintage look that belonged to another era. Really she had wanted a Bri-nylon cardigan, reminiscent of those worn in the 50s that started off a brilliant florescent white then gradually changed with over-washing, because it attracted the dirt, to a matted, yellowing white, or if Daz was used, a blue white. The cardigan that she bought was highly white. It was a bit too white, especially for her, but it was her intention to wear it with an original 50sdress that had been archived in the loft for thirty years but resurrected again because its print was so fashionable at the moment. Catching the bus to the Royal Albert Hall emptied her purse of change and that posed a problem when she needed to phone her son and instead of phoning she asked the security guard where he worked to call him. She asked him to say that his mum was here to take him to lunch. Within moments her hungry son was beside her, ready to go. Over lunch she asked what he had been doing. Well, it was too hard to explain, so he took her back to where he worked to show her.

It was not unusual, when visiting her son, to call in on his place of work to see how he spent his days. She was genuinely interested, but was only a hint nearer to understanding the science behind what he did. Truly, what he did was a complete mystery. It was so utterly big and mysterious that to her, it was like trying to understand the universe and that was partly what he did, try to understand the universe and he did this by generating plasma in a special machine, to simulate what happens in the space beyond the solar-system when there is something like a supernova explosion.

It was eerily quiet. Together they walked down the four flights of stairs to the bowels of Imperial College. Ground Zero was painted in a sunny yellow. Her son pressed the special code into the keypad on the door. In the cavernous room was the hub of the universe. Up the clanking metal stairs and behind a three inch wall of steel was der, der der, der, the vacuum chamber. This was a vast steel core of faultless precision, exquisitely turned on the lathe and one of the most powerful x-ray sources in the world, its solid strength reflected in its argent density. Attached was an array of apparatus and imaging diagnostics, bolted down to withstand the extremes of the experiments, set up to find out, discover and identify what happens when the bright green button was pressed on the control panel.

"So, in simple terms, what have you been doing today?" Basically he was trying to make 'stuff' happen. How he hated being asked that question and he knew his mother would struggle with the complicatedness and complexities of his work. Well, making 'stuff' happen was not a good enough reply and he would have to work much harder before she was satisfied. Well today he had been taking pictures with a special camera called a MCP, which stood for micro-channel plate and this was fixed to the side of the vacuum chamber. She looked through, into the heart of the chamber. She could see a cylinder made of fine wires, made of tungsten or sometimes aluminium, depending on the aim of the experiment, wires thinner than hair, her son showed her a small reel of wire, holding it up to the light so that she could see its fineness and later in the day one million amps, (he talked in millions) of current would pass through the wires for less than a millionth of a second, turning them first to a liquid, then a gas, a metal gas made of metal atoms.

At ten million degrees the gas becomes a charged gas plasma. In the vapour dispersed, the electrons float around freely. A magnetic field pinches itself, pushing the plasma around, ultimately causing the plasma to implode, thought to be, maybe a means to starting of nuclear fusion.

In order to learn how to harness this energy this experiment happens daily and had been doing so for years. It had earned itself the name, "MAGPIE", an acronym for Mega Ampere Generator Plasma Implosion Experiments. By one of the scientists, it was affectionately known as 'The Giant X-ray Light Bulb'. The information was logged and stored on a computer and the data analysed later. The photographic evidence showing the changes that had occurred, was pegged on a line, to dry in a little Perspex box, suspended above the clutter. Everywhere there was clutter. She was assured that it was organised clutter. They clanked down the stairs again and out into the sunny yellow corridor, up the four flights of stairs and out into the April sunshine. She had nothing but admiration for her son and his work, and others in research, who painstakingly worked away, trying to make progress.

Lunch was good and the sit-down better, the workplace tour, enlightening. Leaving her son in search of answers, she walked to Kensington High Street, familiar territory. But it was warm and she had had enough of trying on clothes; whatever she saw, it wouldn't be right and she called it a day. Unlike the morning, it was busy, the pavements cluttered and the roads labouring with hissing air-brakes and blaring sirens and the never ending stream of traffic. After an hour she caught the bus to Green Park to wait for her lift home. As they neared the M25, the sign on the overhead gantry read HEATHROW IS

CLOSED. It was so final, like the world had ended. And indeed, access to the world had. A plume of ash was spewing out of the earth in Iceland and for the next six days there were no bony vertebrae criss-crossing the clear blue sky. The sky was left to the birds.

DREAMS

Her terra aqueous dreams had the fear of a watery grave. They were dark, not dark as in 'can't see', but dark as in 'dark satanic mills'. Unfamiliar with the grass verge she stumbled along and came across a tree, its bare limbs reached out, sculptured like the tree that she had seen years ago in Tate Modern by Dinos and Jake Chapman. It was just there at the edge of a small black pool. Nearby, a man crouched on his haunches, turned. Aware, as she approached, that he was Chinese, it was Burt Kwouk from Last of the Summer Wine. The tree was his fishing rod and although not at all like a conventional fishing rod, she wondered how it could work. It was so cumbersome and unyielding. It looked rigid and firm like a tree trunk yet it was completely hollow, like a rubber mould for clay models, that she remembered making at a friend's house when she was small. His hand reached up and pressed it down into the water then it sprang up again. Returning to the same place the following night, she dreamed again. Hardly a mile from home, she and her friend tried walking where there was more water than land, like a paddy field, but as they stepped onto the visible fringes of grass between the darkening gutters of brackish water, the ground had no strength and they had to pull their feet away quickly before they were swallowed up in the slimy silt. It was disturbing and eerily quiet. In the background the menacing lyrics of Tom Waite's Black Wings was playing over and over and she was reminded of the looming foreboding of the Old Coach Road in Cumbria. Either side of the crunching cinder track, the undergrowth of luring mires and seeping bogs roamed across the great intimidating mass of moorland. Against the desperate wilderness of brown acid peat and sphagnum moss, bright orange lichens sparked in the failing half light. Out of the gloom, the shadowy crumbling ruins of sheepfolds emerged. Now and then a rushing stream spewed out of the ground, dislodging the boulders, spreading over the loose clinker. There was no sign of life or light anywhere. The track went on and on. As the light dwindled, anxiousness was replaced by fear as the blackness of midnight enveloped.

Take an eye for an eye
Take a tooth for a tooth
Just like they say in the Bible
Never leave a trace or forget a face
Of any man at the table
When the moon is a cold chiselled dagger
Sharp enough to draw blood from a stone
He rides through your dreams on a coach
And horses and the fence posts
In the midnight look like bones

Well they've stopped trying to hold him
With mortar, stone and chain
He broke out of every prison
Boots mount the staircase
The door is flung back open
He's not there for he has risen
He's not there for he has risen

Well he once killed a man with a guitar string
He's been seen at the table with kings
Well he once saved a baby from drowning
There are those who say beneath his coat there are wings
Some say they fear him
Others admire him
Because he steals his promise
One look in his eye
Everyone denies
Ever having met him
Ever having met him

He can turn himself into a stranger
Well they broke a lot of canes on his hide
He was born away in a cornfield
A fever beats in his head like a drum inside
Some say they fear him
Others admire him
Because he steals his promise
One look in his eye
Everyone denies
Ever having met him
Ever having met him

His lacerated liquorice larynx sounding like a bad bout of croup, or his throat inflamed, embroidered with ancient nicotine. She dreamed again. It seemed that the footings of the house were part of an irrigation system, fed by rains that fell in the mountains and although she stood on the floor of the sitting room she could clearly see the concrete channels. Suddenly the water came in a torrent, filling up and swirling around, washing over the sides, soaking and darkening the plastered walls. Away from the dreams, in the brightness of day, she believed she could trace back and interpret the imaginary pictures playing in her mind, from the previous day or from the past. (She looked up Dinos and Jake Chapman's tree. It was called Sex. It would be. She liked sexy. The nail polish colour on her toes was called 'Sexy Siren'. It sounded fun. Unlike sexy, the word sex was short and sharp, to the point, it was loud and sounded vulgar and cheap, and didn't have enough syllables. It sounded like its meaning, a there and then activity, functional, which it was, unlike making love which was long and drawn out and sounded deeper and more permanent. However, she didn't think for a moment that where all the creepy-crawlies were reproducing on and in the dead tree, it would be emotional, probably more like a frenetic orgy). What she had difficulty understanding was how it was all the random events got muddled in her imagination to form a dream.

THE UNDERWEAR DEPARTMENT

She left feeling disheartened, blaming the mirrors that threw back the reflection of her mother, the awful rounded back and the dry shrivelling skin that dropped from her bones, wizened and deflated like a spent balloon, discovered long after the party was over. The harsh white light was hardly sympathetic either. Flaws, and freckles, which were as bad, scattered like rust spot on a diseased plant. In the next cubical she overheard the assistant dispensing assurance to a customer saying that nobody would see or know once she was dressed. It was true, but that didn't stop her knowing. All week she tried to stand-up straighter, to lift her chest out of her ribs, feeling in need of a brace to hold herself up. It would not last. Most of the time she ignored her dreadful posture, too busy to notice, too busy to care. Nonetheless the scoliosis was there. Coping with the twist and the curve, her clothes shifted constantly, finding their own level. Obviously she dressed accordingly and avoided clothes that accentuated and revealed, and, like the assistant said, no one would think about what lay beneath. No one noticed. Knowing what to look for, a razor sharp nurse would have seen, pressing her thumb into her forearm, pushing the loose puckered skin into creases, like cooling custard or gravy. It was a simple way of checking for malnutrition or deliberate starvation. For once, longing to turn back the clock, at the time she gave it no thought but now remembered her skin being smooth and full, not fat, but healthy and vital, blemishes insignificant, freckles peppered. Like cracked glaze on well used china, her now her grey withering skin was papery thin the texture of crepe paper once used to make Christmas crackers, and no longer attractive and when she turned the bones in her arm the skin twisted like a skein of thread and dropped in soft folds like polyester crepe cut on the bias. While they hadn't said she guessed that her friends had noticed, but her husband hadn't. As with other things, like the fact that she had worn false eyelashes for an entire fortnight and he hadn't noticed, the feel of her skin, important to him forty years ago went unnoticed or how her watch hung loosely on her wrist, bearing a band of pale skin that had been hidden from the sun. However, he took time to notice and comment on her sister's raw boned thinness, a painful carcass draped in skin, finding herself making excuses for her yet at the same time feeling wounded and betrayed by her husband's concern. Oh, she must stop thinking like that. Life was too short and getting shorter. To save a repeat performance, she bought four bras. Before leaving she browsed in the hosiery department and decided to return to 'American Tan'. She could not understand how this 'natural' shade was favoured by the girls at school, wearing it bravely, she thought, with their little skirts and their ballet pumps, in preference to black, concluding that it was because they were young. This shade, she had abandoned in her teens when coloured and thick denier tights became available. Until then choice had been limited to stockings and all the paraphernalia to hold them up and hold-ups that that inevitably did not. She bought large, not because she was but because she could give them a good hoist without the fear of laddering. Continuing to wear brown and black, the mainstay of the winter, the new tights remained unopened for a couple of weeks. Then, with the sudden burst of summer, she undid one of the slick transparent envelopes. Not believing for a moment that her own legs would look like the lovely long legs adorning the packaging, she took them out, unwrapping the filmy gossamer as she did from their cardboard frame. She threaded her hand through the delicate cobweb of fibres to the shapely foot, carefully drawing it over her toes and winding round the heel of her great Ramesses foot. She was not the least surprised at the appearance. They were her mother's legs, inherited, thick and stout, russeted and knotted with varicose veins, mighty waterlogged ankles, sturdy and shapeless like elephant's legs, better covered in black sixty-denier Lycra. And she liked elephants, they were loyal and dependable, they just kept going and she loved their babies, they had such personality. Standing around in front of the mirror she considered the image of her legs from all different views and from all different angles and different heights, because everybody was a different height and looked from a different angle. Holding another mirror she checked to see how they looked from the back. And people did look. Remembering Tony, who commented on the glinting hairs sprouting through the mesh of Joan's tights while having his cup of coffee, telling all and sundry how disgusted he was. People didn't realize how lucky they were to have flawless skin and smooth brown shapely legs. Like her mother's, the thin undernourished surface of her skin was covered in hairline cracks as fine as those on old porcelain and typical of those with a fair auburn complexion. Through the filmy 'American Tan' she could see the parched earth, the pale dimpled cellulite and every type of vein, the bubbling distended ones that meandered, the thin ones like biro lines that crisscrossed the continents of flesh and livid clusters of broken veins that looked like bruises or those like the Ganges Delta that fanned out behind her left knee. There were blotches of freckles and brown moles mottled her bone, goose pimpled skin. In certain lights, even after fifty years, a sock line remained, where, until she was twelve, elastic had pressed-in and dented. Above the line, the skin was rougher and tougher, acclimatized to the wroth of winter, when quite literally the epidermis turned blue in the cold. It was only her who was so aware and so against 'nylons'. To improve their appearance she had taken to using moisturising lotion with a sun-kissed look, which was fine until she had her legs waxed and it all came off on the waxing strip. In the summer she preferred bare legs, but not hers, she didn't like the thought of people seeing them, the light catching a stray hair, they might be repulsed, like her mother's legs used to repulse her. She too wore 'American Tan', but in substantial 30 denier, and bought them in packs of five. She remembers the dense choking smell of unwashed tights, like the smell a piece of lamb before it gets going in the oven, and seeing patches of dead flaking cells, like scurf, sloughed off by the Lycra, caught in creases and the gingery discolouration, where her big sweaty, pasty calloused feet had rubbed and brown polish from her shoes had stained. Seeing her tights scrunched up and ready to wash reminded her of when she and her sister cleared their mother's house and there were tights everywhere, stuffed into drawers, under cushions, behind the bed, pulled off with relief, discarded and forgotten. The awful memory of it all was enough to put her off.

Nothing was happening. There were no letters. There were no emails. All had gone quiet. The uncertainty of waiting to hear about her manuscript was unnerving. She was quietly hungry for news. Then, when she was least expecting it, there was a letter on the mat, thanking her for being patient and yes, the publishers were interested.

Her mother had died in April 2006 and she remembered how in the summer that followed she had idly opened the small leather case that had belonged to her father. Along with other things it had been stored in her mother's trunk, below the desk in her son's room, now transformed into an office. The desk, at least 6ft 6ins, was built under the window where his bed used to be and took care of her sewing machine and the computer, printer, etc. In the trunk were odds and ends, a chiming clock, her father's kilt and accessories, a pair of flowery curtains; not her cup of tea, but too good to throw away, and the brown leather case.

The trunk had been there several years but it was not until her mother had died that her curiosity got the better of her and she succumbed to looking inside the case. Remembering it once, being under her parent's bed, she seemed to think that it was in the corner wardrobe when she and her sister found it, accidentally ripping the leather in their impatient frenzy to get it open, hoping to find wads of money and laughing when they found nothing more than boring bits of paper. Snapping it shut again, it was placed in the trunk and forgotten until that summer.

She wondered if her mother had ever been tempted to look once her husband had died and hoped that she hadn't. Her hurt would have been unbearable. Maybe her mother did know and couldn't face the complicated confusion and terrible guilt. She would never know for sure. Inside the case was a secret world, which until that moment she had been unaware. Somehow it didn't feel right, prying into things that were not hers. On her hands and knees she carefully removed the small black and white photos and the letters and the documents, slowly turning them over in her hands, reading the scrawled handwriting on the thin yellowing pages, opening them, refolding them, returning them to the pockets in the lid of the case. The revelation of the contents of the case shocked and made her realize how little she had known. In disbelief she looked all over again. Immersed, time slipped quietly by. One particular photograph interested her more than any other. She called it 'the boy in the square photograph'.

The black and white photograph was square and small, 2 x 2 ins. It showed a little boy in shorts and striped tee-shirt. He had a cheeky grin and his hair was plastered down with what looked like Brylcreem. In the background was a galvanized metal water butt. She estimated that he was more or less the same age as her and like her assumed him to be very much alive. But where? Who was the boy who had been so carefully protected in the pocket of her father's case for sixty years? Since that day she had tried to find out.

Inside the case was all about her father's life before the life with her mother. Fifty years of life. There were numerous pictures, photos and newspaper clippings about his regiment and this had prompted her to send to Glasgow for his army record. Months and months later it arrived. From that she found that he was one of eight siblings and more interestingly that he already had a family of eight children and that he had married in 1920 and not until 1980 was he divorced. Meanwhile, in the case there was memorabilia, ration books, two savings books, his passport, unused, things to do with the Masons, his divorce papers, his birth certificate and some photos. Most of the things were interesting to pick up and look at. And in the four years she had done that often, trying to look for answers beyond the facts, boring into the frail yellowing paper, hovering the magnifying glass over the photos, so small in those days, trying to gauge how it all happened.

The discovery of another family prompted her to go to Scotland and find them. And she did. Life for them had gone on, unaware of what her father, their father too, had done. All they knew was that he had upped and left their mother in 1946, leaving her to bring them all up.

She came across a savings book. Between 1946 and 1950 her father had saved a few shillings regularly in a Post Office savings account, the date stamps were Stenhousemuir, Kings Langley, Hemel Hempstead, and Watford and when the book was updated, the address was her own. This intrigued her and she wanted to know who he was and where he was. She contacted the Birth, Deaths and Marriages offices, firstly in London, without success, then in Edinburgh. She sent for his birth certificate and that confirmed that the D stood for Donald and that his father was her father and that he had been born in Stirling. She had another half-brother. Where was he? Donald's mother was Dorothy Verrall, and there was a very extensive family tree of the family, twelve pages long and amongst the many names was her father's, listed as being married to Dorothy Lillian Verrall and below, the name of their son, Donald, born in 1946.

Here was another family. On Donald's birth certificate was her father's signature. From this information and addresses and postmarks and places where he was during the war, she tried to piece together her father's whereabouts.

She had assumed the photograph to be the newly found Donald but soon realised when she finally made contact with him that it wasn't. Neither was it any of her many half brothers and sisters in Scotland.

Joining Genes Reunited the following year allowed her to

try and find out about the artefacts in the case. It was a slow laborious process and trails often lead nowhere. At times she lost heart, at times she felt frustrated and wanted to give up. Besides joining the family history web site she tried to discover information by writing letters and making phone calls.

Most recently the *Daily Mail* ran a feature called 'Missing and Found'. It was worth a try and she drew up a time-line and emailed it along with the photograph. She wrote.

For over three years I have been trying to find out who the boy in the photograph is.

Through the search I have discovered two separate families inextricably linked together by my father Jonathan Weir, born in Denny Stirlingshire in 1902 and died in Luton, Bedfordshire in 2000.

It is a very complicated story and until 2006 I knew nothing about my father.

He was married to Margaret Harrison in 1920 and they had eight children. He was in the Argyle and Southerland Highlanders then the Royal Warwickshire Reg.

Officially he left his first family in 1946 and set up home with Dorothy Verrall (who was visiting Europe from Australia). They had one son, Donald. Various documents implied that they were married. Dorothy told her son that they were married on a day trip to France. Dorothy and her son returned to Australia on the *Arcadia* in September 1949. Dorothy worked for a family in Birmingham as a nanny. She looked after twin boys, Thomas and William born in 1935 with the surname Black. They lived at 175 Lightwoods Road, Bearwood, Birmingham. Dorothy Verrall arrived on 28 April 1937 in Hull.

My father met my mother towards the end of the 40s. They

both worked at Abbots Hill School in Kings Langley Herts. She left to have me at The Haven in Yateley. Some time later they were together again and set up home together as Mr and Mrs. My sister was born in 1953.

In 1980 my mother and father were finally married because Margaret and Jonathan were divorced.

The photograph intrigues me because it was kept with my father's things and obviously meant something to him. Knowing the sort of man he was I am quite sure that the boy is another half-brother. His clothing and look could be that of the late fifties/sixties. Maybe the man, by now, in his late fifties/sixties will already have this photo and will recognise himself. His mother might still be alive and she might have the photo.

I have no names to go on but have areas in the country where my father lived and approximate dates.

Bedfordshire Eaton Bray, Totternhoe 1952 – 2000

Stirlingshire Denny 1902-1945

Warwickshire Gaydon 1945 Snowhill Birmingham 1945

Stirlingshire Stenhousemuir 1947

Hertfordshire Watford 1948 Kings Langley 1949 Hemel Hempstead 1950

A letter was redirected to my father c/o Mrs L Humphries, 3 Lighthorne Cottages Banbury Road Nr Warwick in 1945.

A passport was issued to my father in August 1949 (I wonder if he was going to go to Australia with Dorothy and Donald).

There is a letter dated November 1951 from Abbots Hill School.

I am hoping that you will be able to help.

Within days the reply via email was back. Rejection again. The office received thirty requests a week from people asking to feature their Missing stories and with only space for one they were unable to help, but suggested Gill Whitley. Without a name she couldn't help either. How could she find out? She typed. "How can I find someone without a name?" Google threw up some sites to contact. It surprised her that there were any, but how would she know if they were genuine?

FRIENDS

Seeing their dear friends destroying each other with words was heartbreaking. They were doting parents and had devoted their lives to their two daughters. The enormous pressure of maintaining the work/life balance, coping with the demands of families and relationships and the inevitability of creeping old age, all the time fighting against the slow deterioration seemed to outweigh any pleasure that they once shared with each other. Her friend was the most wonderful mother. Her pure unremitting love was faultless. Never tiring of her responsibility she was constantly available to their beck and call. Always putting her children first, she had left herself behind, paling into insignificance, no longer needing to make decisions, no longer required. She had clung to her daughters, nurtured them, willing them to be successful, interested in all they did. They had their mother's undivided attention. The relentless sacrifice had crushed her confidence. The effort of it all had left its mark. And when her husband subjected her to a barrage of instructions, she was too worn out, no longer having the energy to fight back, to stand her ground. From taking the skin off the mushrooms to hovering dust he barked the orders and expected them carried out at once. His behaviour was appalling and it saddened her to see her long-suffering friend belittled, patiently bearing the provocation. That is how pure she was. In his bullying way he had made her into a nervous wreck, making her totally dependent on him. Of course her husband had not always been like that. At times he was how she remembered him, fun-loving, warm and generous, but his unpredictability, his Jekyll and Hyde personality was unpleasant and out of character. Seeing these uncomfortable episodes made her think. It made her husband think too. Preferring to wait until they were driving home, he had said nothing. He did not recognize himself, he could not see his own foibles.

The twelfth had arrived. The long awaited date. The 'glorious twelfth'. The date when England played their first match in the 2010 World Cup. All day she messed about in the kitchen preferring to cook all the things she hadn't had time to make the previous weekend. Well in fact two things, interesting tarts with onions as a key ingredient were really left over from Christmas because the feta cheese had been bought then and its date was about to expire. On Friday she had written a list of all the things she wanted to make, feta and red onion tart was one of them. Like the twelfth, the twenty-second had rolled round surprisingly quickly. The feta cheese had sat in the fridge for six months. It seemed to her that the whole country wanted to sit down at 7.30 p.m. and watch the match. Earlier in the day she had collected her son from the station and that short journey seemed fraught with dangers, as though people were anxious to be back in time. Nothing was going to stop them. Even herself, who was not in the least interested in the sport, was caught up in the furore. Tesco was awash with advertising the big event. They didn't need much excuse. Mobile fridges had been added to the existing fridges, cluttering up the gangways, there to catch your eye and trip you up as you steered the labouring trolley around the already crowded store. They made you think, in case you forgot, that you really did need the grab bags and the Stellas for the boy's night in, in front of the television. Goal posts, complete with nets, were constructed over the ends of freezers. Goals worth having, in the net. Flags were draped from the ceiling and turf was stuck to the floor. The crowd cheered from huge TVs at the entrance and suited staff huddled, talking tactics. For the duration, which for England might not be long, she decided to support the South African economy by buying South African wine. That was her contribution. A crucial game on a Wednesday afternoon allowed for a shortened day, three quarters of an hour shorter. Lunch time was greatly reduced and the five minute walk time between lessons was removed to enable this to happen. The whole country sighed with relief, England moved forward to the next round. The St George's flags attached to car roofs were still there, frayed edges beginning to show, limply fluttering. The car park as usual was rammed, the hostile white heat of the afternoon claiming her energy. Dazzling sunlight reflected, stabbing and glinting on glass and metal. Speculation combined with uncertainty continued until 3 p.m. on Sunday. The media armed with facts and statistics were relentless. With quickening urgency once again the whole country got ready to watch. She, like many others uninterested in the game, sat in the garden. Gently the trees soughed and apart from the soft pattering of leaves in the warm wafting air and the occasional car passing, everything was quiet. Above, the ever-changing sky. Just before half-time a combined cheer went up from nearby houses, doors and windows wide open in the recent hot spell, people spilling into the gardens with their beers, one eye on the television newly fixed to the wall. Although that was good she was conscious of a heavy uneasy silence, spoiling the entertainment. How they ached for their team to win. Disgraced, the England team bowed out. The papers showed no mercy and neither did the fans. By Monday morning the fraying fluttering antennae attached to car roofs in the car park on Friday afternoon had been discarded in disgust.

The wild smell of wool pervaded. Tufts of raw fleece had been ripped out of their thick matted coats where they had rubbed against the barbed wire fence. She had collected it to show the streetwise pupils, who knew nothing of wool, hoping to generate some understanding of the countryside. They were not interested in her bag of dirty flea ridden fibres. They didn't want to touch the wool and feel its waxy coarseness or spin it with their fingers. She pictured the flocks grazing on the drizzly uplands one minute, then bleating and baaing in the sheering shed waiting for their dirty wool to be removed in one clever coat, the next. How many fleeces had made the new carpets that paved her floor?

Although it shouldn't be, talking about birds was an 'age' thing. Increasingly birds featured in their lives. Of course they always had, but not usually in general conversation, as they did now. And although not ornithologists, they had a number of bird books, referring to them every now and then when they needed to check a warbler or a finch. All the time the birds were twittering and chirping and cooing and cheeping and trilling and calling and tweeting and singing. Only when a predator approached did a hushed silence fall. It was like flicking a light switch, all the small birds stopped chirping at once. In the hedges they held their breaths until the brush with danger passed. Unaware of her, a sparrow hawk silently turned in one quick movement under the pergola with a collared dove firmly in its grasp. Landing only feet away on the coarse dry grass, it mercilessly proceeded to peck and stab and claw at the half dead bird until it fell limp and breathless from trying to struggle free from the savage attack and the inevitable brutal death. Now and then the hawk stopped its frenzy and listened, not once relinquishing its powerful grip on the soft body of the bird. Feathers stirred faintly as the hawk, feeling restored enough to move it again to the safety of the undergrowth, clutched at its carrion and flew low along the path to the end of the garden. Occasionally, a solitary grey heron stole the show. Standing poised and slender, motionless beside the pond he looked ornamental. Elegantly bending his fine brown bony legs he silently and deliberately placed his splayed feet into the grass, all the time risking exposure, his eyes remaining alert to danger, i.e. when she ran outside clapping her hands, immediately he sprung and was airborne, his slow lethargic flapping like a massive pterodactyl, curved away from the garden, banking skyward, his legs trailing behind. Her husband could identify the differences between a rook, a jackdaw and a crow and would explain to her in detail about their beaks and she would nod her head in understanding.

On freezing winter days her husband launched into making bird boxes and soon one was fixed to the pergola. Usually the blue tits sought shelter in the shrubs, blending with the variegation but the anticipation of them house hunting, looking inside, going inside, looking around then looking out was so distracting. They even took photos. Worried that the circumference of the hole was too small, her husband checked the size for blue tits, removed the box and increased it by a millimetre. And even funnier was when a blue tit clung to the nearby thermometer as though he was checking the temperature. Spellbound, they would watch the box in the spring when the eggs had hatched and could hear the chicks' high frequency tweeting increasing to such a pitch until the frazzled parents delivered grubs to their gapping beaks, temporarily subduing their clamouring offspring. And, when the broods, and there were two nest boxes simultaneously full of chicks at each end of the garden, began to fledge, her husband became anxious for their safety and promised for next year to construct a cradle made out of branches to soften their fall. Everywhere there were pigeons and they flapped their wings like sheets on a line on a windy day. Their numbers had increased dramatically in recent years, which in her opinion was not commendable. Plumped up like airships they bumbled about the grass, pecking and she could hear them as loud as humans as their claws slipped trying to grip on the kitchen roof. She would duck to dodge them, as they swooped to land and even when perched on the chimney, their boring coo, could be heard in the sitting room, above the noise of the television. Bring back pigeon pie. Out of nowhere a posse of starlings descended. Hot-headed, noisy and gregarious the wide-boys were back in town. Strutting about on the grass like spivs, looking cool, or thought they did, each outdoing the other, lean and hungry, looking for action, looking for trouble, looking for worms. If the starlings drove cars, they would stand back to admire the latest wheel trims or the spoiler, music pumping. Leaving the garden in peace, the smooth operators were gone. She could see what was going to happen as soon as she saw the blackbird taking a chance, flying low across the dual carriageway. The car in front hit the bird. In slow motion it was propelled into the air. Soft black feathers spiralled, floating gently in the draught and continued to lift and flutter long after the car behind crushed the blackbird beyond recognition. Magpies, seizing an opportunity, chancing their luck and dicing with death, hopped around impatiently on the central reservation, anxiously waiting and risking all, eager to pick and peck at the bloody entrails smeared across the road. She remembered her mother doffing her hat if she saw a magpie. They brought a smile and had such a showy confidence. In another country you would be thrilled to see such a conspicuous flamboyant bird, pied black, glossy iridescent feathers cutting a dashing sight in his stylish tuxedo, full of raucous chatter and rattling chak-chak-chak. And there were rhymes. 'One for sorrow, two for mirth. Three for a wedding, four for birth.' And so on. Like pigeons they used to be part of the rural scene, sitting on the backs of sheep pecking at the ticks in their fleece but now urban dwellers, hanging about in the apple tree at the end of the garden, waiting to steal the baby blackbirds from the nest in the newly constructed flower pot rack at the back of the shed, when the mother left in search of food, or perched, sharp-eyed, panning the vicinity for gold or silver, a bottle top or maybe her earring, lost in the garden while weeding a fortnight ago, it would make an ideal chandelier and give its cat's cradle of a nest a touch of glamour. There had always been blackbirds in the garden. They were related and like many families, how they argued, disagreements broke out regularly and all hell was let loose. She remembered one, born with its foot facing the opposite way, a flash of white in its wing. For want of a better name he was known as Hoppy. And even though the young were fluffed out as big as moorhens, bigger than their mother, she was fiercely protective, flapping and calling with all she could muster. Alert to the insistence of any boisterous commotion in the garden they would go outside and check for cats or the hawk or a magpie. They liked nothing better than to sift through the dead leaves looking for grubs, flicking them as they did so onto the path, then she would listen to her husband scolding as he took the yard broom, sweeping them back into the undergrowth again or fasten on to a worm, tugging and pulling with her beak, stretching it like a rubber band until it pinged from the earth when she would bite it into pieces and fly to the open mouths in her nest. Even before the sun fell over the garden the blackbirds would feast on the ripening raspberries, swinging along the canes not content to consume a whole berries, which she would have been happy about, but to leave half eaten fruit that was no good to her. The dearest little wren, a round, brown ball of a bird, darted from one side of the paved area, (some would call it the patio, but to her it was the slabs) to the other, hiding in the safety of the shrubs, it didn't go looking for trouble. It was her favourite. Once a common sight and making a come-back the thrush too visited occasionally, its song filling the air, stopping long enough for her to admire its proud speckled chest while it repeatedly bashed the life out of the snails that looked like humbugs, on the path. And the robin too, dependable, always there at the end of her elbow when she was weeding, his head on one side, listening, quietly waiting for her to finish. And of course there were sparrows, busying themselves, endlessly twittering about nothing in particular, petty disputes breaking out all the time in the concrete tenement of the screen wall over a crust of dry bread dropped carelessly by a passing bird en route to somewhere else or squabbling over which wooden balcony of the trellis they would perch and sun themselves or making little dust craters in the dry warm soil or noisily making untidy open plan nests in the gutter above the kitchen window or mindlessly tear at her yellow crocuses as soon as they sparked into life. On sultry August afternoons their eggs would hatch and smoky plumes of flying ants would open their lacy wings to dance in the sunlight. Their lives were short lived however as the sparrows clumsily pretending to be humming birds took advantage of the ready meal, catching the dizzy wisps of flying ants on the wing or afterwards when she had boiled them alive with a kettle of water, lazily pecking the dead bodies from the gritty funeral pyres between the slabs. Stumpy was a house sparrow and lived in the garden amongst the flowerpots. He/she had no tail feathers, thus his/her name and due to lack of exercise was prone to being a little overweight. He/she had a mate called Stumpy's Mate. Like an old married couple, they were always together, hopping about, finding food. Joy. Yes, the 'outside space' was the place to be.

ECHOES

The warm swirling air lifted the lightness of her dress and she would brush it down again with the palm of her hand. Arriving home, the sun still high, she would turn the chair to face it and sit with a cup of tea. Languid. Closing her eyes against the hostile white light, her mind swarming with the congestion of the day, she would fall asleep. Reminders of a year ago were all around, digging the dreamy new potatoes from the warm crumbly soil, the dry prickly lawn, watering the thirsty pots, eating outside and sitting outside in the fading light, stargazing and bat watching, finding the remainder of the day soothing before the airless nights when sleep would not come. So too did clouded skies remind her, of when she was confined to the overcrowded house on those long, drab, silent afternoons. Even Sam and Ellen appeared again in *Remember Me.*

She lay in a narrow furrow on the edge of the land reserved for wildlife, listening to the rhythm of the night. Her husband sprawled across the rest of the bed, his breathing like gathering thunder, a great bale of covers wedged between them. Except for a chink to let in the glow from the streetlight, the curtains were closed. Doors and windows were open to allow a through draught and all the time the pleated fullness of the curtains would bend and crimp, darkening shadows pressing against the window, their hems dragging on the sill, then abruptly straightening out, then dragging on the sill, sweeping in and out, in and out, brushing earrings and lipsticks, carelessly left, onto the floor in cushioned thuds. Now and then the curtains would unexpectedly billow out into the room, reaching towards her, calling her, come and play, come and play, flapping and twirling on themselves to be sucked in the next gust, out of the window, into the night. An occasional car passed and in the background the mesmerising sea of trees heaved.

She knew that until she confronted him she would not settle. He sat absentmindedly watching an old football match on the big screen in the corner of the sitting room, the sound at mute. Moving into the large space beside him on the settee, she tentatively began. "Tell me." She said. She wrote rapidly on a stark white sheet of A4 paper, the thought of filling its emptiness, daunting, wondering, as she began how far she would get. There was an awkward silence. At first he was reluctant. He found it hard to think about it. It was all so long ago. Not being treated fairly was quickly followed by the fact that he didn't get a football when he was five. She had heard that before. Not satisfied with one sentence covering his entire childhood, she gently plumbed the depths the of his past, his past before her, carefully removing each layer, trying, in her head to fit the pieces together. His father had no time for him. He was completely disinterested in his son's love of football and fishing and cricket. He played for numerous teams, but not once did he go to support and cheer him on, like the other dads. The hurt of it all still wounded. As far as he was concerned, his son was there to help him with the old cars that he fixed, holding a spanner or cleaning rust from a bumper with wire wool, not asking his sister, because she was a girl and not asking or rather telling his brother because he was too busy being clever. She had heard that before too. He didn't want his son to work with a shovel. Is that how he saw him? She had suspected this for a long time but admitting it to her was daring. Limiting his answers to short stunted sentences he was loathed to elaborate and make a paragraph. Using her memories of the road, the house and the garden she could imagine how it was, him, waiting and watching through the half-nets in the bay window for his father to return from work on his bike. His bike, the bike that his mother had scrimped and saved for, for him, the sound of the back gate opening and closing on the rough concrete and the bike being leaned against the wall, then, avoiding his father at all cost, quietly let himself out of the gate and peddle to freedom without a backward glance. At times he needed prompting to get him going again. She could hear anger and frustration in his voice and tried not to look at him, not wanting to see his pain. If she had lost her composure, she would have dissolved into tears and the opportunity to talk would have passed. He didn't look at her, continuing instead to stare at the TV. There was little his mother could do to protect him against her husband's quick temper and short fuse. Answering back or refusing to help only resulted in being punished. Struggling with one hand to hold on to his squirming son, he would loosen the belt around his waist and thrash and thrash until his body surrendered sobbing. It was not uncommon for Ukrainian fathers or any fathers for that matter, to beat their children and their wives. Some even locked their children in cupboards. And even though the fathers were the ogres, the mothers, often at their wit's end were also to blame, threatening, "Just you wait till your father comes home".

When he was eight, he ran away. Beyond what is now the kitchen was a ramble of rough brick outhouses and behind the buildings her husband and his brother built a hutch without mortar, out of all the odd bricks left lying around in the garden. For ten hours he crouched on the mud floor, undiscovered in the hutch.

Although unsure at first, he took to school. People began to take an interest in him. He took on responsibilities, like rubbing dubbin into the boots before a game of football and keeping the score for the cricket matches at the rec. His PE teacher Mr Roberts, asked him which foot he kicked with. "Right, sir." "Left back it is then." And so, from the beginning he learnt to kick equally well with both feet, a tale fondly remembered each time a premier player kicked and missed with the wrong foot. It was expected that pupils had an apron for woodwork, without one meant that they could not participate in the practical lesson. Disappointed, her husband didn't have an apron and when he got home from school, he proceeded without delay to make one using a torn-up sheet, hand stitched with clumsy tacks and crude over-sewing. Feeling a mixture of shame and embarrassment he bravely wore the rudimentary apron until a new one cold be afforded. Like the steel-toed work shoes that he wore for a term acquired from his father because there was no money for Clarks or Start-rite school shoes. They were not close and although the fear of his father was always there, he had no choice but to get on with it. He was a sulking, miserable man and when in the heat of summer and the tension of visitors arriving from the Ukraine was at breaking point he launched the ironing board out of the house and into the pond. A bitter exchange ensued and her husband lashed out at his father "I'm big and you're small and you can't hit me now." Quelled, his father said nothing. Surprisingly, when a stroke disabled him, her husband felt sorry for his disagreeable father in his old age. When it was all too late he cried, saying that he was sorry. Her husband did not believe him, he was feeling sorry for himself. As they sat his memories turned to when he was really small, growing-up in the camp, an ex WRAF billet, a circus of children running about, free and feral. Friendships endured and when they met up in later years, their early experiences bound them together.

Sensitive to his feelings she cautiously continued, bravely approaching the guarded territory of their life together. What he did say was that he liked their easy-going independence that they shared, each allowing each other their freedom. He did what he wanted and so did she. She was silent and did not entirely agree. While that seemed to be good now, it hadn't always been like that and she reminded him of all the times he went fishing when the children were small, hardly in the house, the car was packed and he was gone. Some wives would not be so accommodating, not allowing their husbands to go, insisting that they shared everything together. She felt that she had been a good wife. Sometimes however, she felt relief when he left to go to work or fishing or to the allotment where, until vandals decapitated a fine parade of resplendent January King cabbages, leaving them to rot, he dug and hoed for the pleasure, it could be anything from a couple of hours to twelve hours at least until he returned. Slipping into a relaxed mode the tension would subside. Nothing seemed to matter anymore. She would enjoy reading another chapter or another story to the children at bedtime, or scratch around in the Lego case with them looking for a blue arm, without the pressure. Suddenly, he just said what annoyed him about her. He couldn't stand her generalizing statements and the way she came out with her sweeping accusations, which he felt were magnified and exaggerated, unjust and uncalled for. She admitted that she was guilty of using the word always rather than the word sometimes.

Hesitantly she asked him why he had felt uncertain in the first few years of their marriage, why he didn't believe that she would stay with him. After a long pause, he said, it was because she had started to spread her wings and fly, that she was going abroad with her job, visiting exciting places, and he was not part of that, he didn't know what she was doing, or who she was with. Unlike nowadays when girls and boys mingle freely and even different ages interact. In those days, girls talked to girls and boys talked to boys. A girl talking to a boy meant only one thing. He worried about his unsociable shift pattern and that she spent long nights on her own. She told him that he had had, no need to worry. She had it all.

Pressing on, she said to him that she didn't think that he thought, that he didn't notice how very sad she had been at times. He said that she was an important part in his life and that he couldn't live without her. For her, she saw that as him avoiding taking responsibility for himself. It was just as well that he said. "I don't think we should go any further." A greying patina fell over his face. With that, she called it a day and although there was nothing really that she had not heard before, she had not got rattled and grabbed the headlines, to end embroiled in an argument. Her voice had remained steady. She had been calmly subjective and felt that she had made some progress. It had left her thirsty.

Days later, over a glass of red wine, (left-over South African), he told her about the lodgers. Although their house was big and roomy, a far cry from the camp arrangements, they all slept in one room, leaving others free for lodgers. Always an opportunist, his father saw it as doing them a favour and earning a few bob for himself. Her husband didn't like those transient people, those lodgers who stayed at his house, remembering one building a car out of aluminium and another, a Hungarian, who regularly cooked up a goulash in their meagre room that they called the kitchen.

He had one friend, more than any other, with whom he sought solace. His name was Peter. His friend's father, Mr Meadows kept a small chicken farm and her husband liked nothing more than to collect the eggs, wash them and grade them, much to Mrs Meadows's delight as it saved her the job. Mrs Meadows looked like the Queen. She was gentle and quietly spoken. Her husband was introduced to the mini-meal, called elevenses, and to meringues and fruit cake at tea-time and his friend's parents were the proud owners of a fridge and so, when it was hot he enjoyed home-made orange lollies made in aluminium moulds, so cold that they would stick to his lips. After fighting in the desert during the war, Mr Meadows had come home via Italy and nicknamed the boys, Pedro and Roberto. Until he had a bike, her husband had walked the few miles to Peter's house. They were never in, preferring to play outside in the numerous barns and sheds, melting lead into nuggets for target practice and making fires and burning asbestos. With an air-rifle they used to shoot at the mice in the meal house and pick peas for Mrs Meadows and look for mushrooms. To her husband this unfamiliar 'English' way of life was so removed from his own. Life went on without the continual fighting and arguing and abuse. Sundays were the longest of days, the days when it was not respectable to visit. Even though the farm has long gone, he goes to where his friend still lives to remember those days, those precious summer days, growing up with the freedom to play, without the threat of being made to work on the cars in the yard, without being put-upon. How, in those early years did they befriend each other? She imagined that they sat next to each other, doing their sums, hundreds, tens, and units neatly in the squares of the little exercise book and drawing pictures with stubby wax crayons and writing a sentence about "My Day Out" with a blunt pencil, sitting in their short trousers and their checked winceyette shirts, buttoned to the neck, sleeveless jumpers for extra warmth, socks held up with knotted elastic that dug deeply behind the knees and that itched like mad when they were removed, playing according to the seasons, jacks or marbles on sunny days or playing conkers or lining-up to wait their turn on the long icy slide crossing the playground at break-time. Her husband had started school with only a smattering of English. How did he fair? Her husband could not remember. It was blanked out, erased from his deep black ocean of memories.

A DAY OUT

It was a rare sight and a privilege seeing the red kite. After years of being given a bad press the raptor had been reintroduced and was once again regaining its territory, hugging the downs, hanging in the wind that swept the side of the Chilterns from the west, the grass held flat to the chalky earth in silky waves. Its beady eyes scanned carefully, painstakingly covering ground, scavenging for the remains of a decaying carcass to pick at. It was all the more special because it was so unexpected, unlike the wild animals that they did expect to see at the zoo. They had stopped to look over the glacial valley, to spot familiar landmarks. Gulping air, their voices were lost in the wind. She had hankered after going to the zoo again for a while. And so out-of-the-blue they went one Saturday morning. Of course it was not the same as it used to be. They would say that. For one thing, it did not seem so big and the animals had been moved about and were not where they remembered them to be. The wolves used to menacingly pace along the perimeter fence, visible from the road and the elephants used to be trumpeting at the entrance; there used to be polar bears and lions in deep pits, guarded with spiky topped fencing. The overgrown remains of the old pits where they once lived looked like archaeological digs, waiting to be discovered. Animal welfare had improved massively in recent times, giving the animals more respect and allowing much more freedom in their houses and pens. George, the newest elephant, born in April, stole her heart. He was just delightful and did all the elephant things, like holding his mother's tail with his trunk and sheltering close, protected in her shadow. Undoubtedly, she had a soft spot for baby elephants

On leaving downstairs for bed her husband lingered on the two lovely pictures, pictures of their wonderful sons, one taken after the special marriage of her niece on that winter afternoon and the other taken, where it hung now, in the dining room after the traditional Christmas Eve feast, when a whole years worth of anticipation and excitement was contained in those few hours and before too many beers sapped their energy, spoiling their lovely smiles, their beautiful teeth and the promising expectation of youth. He battled constantly for times past, wondering where it had all gone and no longer at the core of it, no longer actively making it happen, seeing it grow. God, he was sentimental.

Like her friend, she was too accommodating. From her mother she had learnt how to keep the peace and keep her husband, without the need to say that it was for the best. She didn't find herself arguing or sticking up for herself. Instead she had gradually become complacent and indifferent. She should have complained and expressed her displeasure rather than suppressing her thoughts and disguising her feelings. Over the years, she had allowed this to happen. She had lacked confidence and self-esteem. It was her that was to blame for the built-up silence and the eventual failure, not her husband. Done so, for good reason, for it was her who had, over the years deceived, stolen the truth, made a good job of masking her feelings, backing down, putting-up with, letting things go, to keep the peace. With the slightest hint of assertion, or lack of co-operation or difference of opinion, in her mind their relationship deteriorated. She had to make a point of ignoring or concealing things that riled and annoyed her, falsely pretending that they didn't. Surely that was what she had nearly always done.

She was always looking for things to share with him, but increasingly, she did things on her own, simply because he didn't want to. She doubted that he would voluntarily participate in one of her interests and he did not reciprocate or instigate things that could be shared and enjoyed together. Preoccupied with children and all that they entailed it was easy to drift into obscurity. She was just someone who did what was necessary to make life comfortable, a convenience. Like her mother was a convenience to her husband.

When she was young, she had been ambitious, striving and feeling guilty for wanting more, more than what was on offer for a girl like her. Working in a shop or a factory or a hairdressers were basically the options and in no time at all she would be pushing a pram, so what was the point in filling her head with fancy ideas. He had held her back. Not saying that she couldn't do something or other but that he made her feel uncomfortable about her choices. And so she succumbed to appease him, gave in, like her mother would have done. He was thinking of himself. He had been told as much by one of her teachers, long retired, with whom they had kept in touch, over the years.

Apart from her name she had written nothing on the 11 exam paper. Even now she could see where she sat in the hall, towards the end of the back row. Her mother once said how irritated she felt about being sat in alphabetical order and although she had not thought about it before she could see that going from a 'W' to a 'B' when she married, was an advantage. Along with her very clever friend who had also failed the dreaded 11 but had done outstandingly well, way beyond the realms of academia, she left what was known as the "secondary modern school" for the "girl's grammar" down the road and on leaving there, she went to college, where she threw herself into making and doing all the things that were in those days part of the teacher training programme. It lasted no more than ten weeks. It was her husband who missed her so much, who wanted her to be there when he needed her. Saying goodbye at Rugby station until the next time was too much for him. "She came back because of you". Her teacher said to her husband. In her opinion, love, and she assumed it to be so then, would stand the test of time. She was so sure, then. Filled with a blind confidence, she thought that she knew everything that there was to know. Looking back, she knew nothing when she was young. Again, in her head she was singing, or trying to sing, 'I Vow to Thee My Country'.

I vow to thee, my country, all earthly things above,
Entire and whole and perfect, the service of my love:
The love that asks no question, the love that stands the test,

That lays upon the altar the dearest and the best;
The love that never falters, the love that pays the price,
The love that makes undaunted the final sacrifice.

And there's another country, I've heard of long ago,
Most dear to them that love her, most great to them that know;
We may not count her armies, we may not see her King;
Her fortress is a faithful heart, her pride is suffering;
And soul by soul and silently her shining bounds increase,
And her ways are ways of gentleness and all her paths are peace.

And it did stand the test of time. He was truly dependable. He was always there in the background. Nothing short of rock solid stability surrounded her, his security provided for her, a bedrock, a foundation, from which she had the freedom to do practically anything, where she could nurture her rash of lofty ideas. Routinely, various impulsive ventures from her wild emporium of grand ideas materialized in her imagination, sourcing components, manufacturing, promoting, distributing and retailing. She would invest in property, renovate, change its use, open a shop or open a tea-room. To her, anything was possible. Her crazy pipedreams and wild desires, however, remained in her head. He kept her anchored firmly to the seabed, the relentless swell of ideas washed around her, now and then threatening to bubble to the surface. What he was not prepared to do was to share the risk and without his support every step-of-the-way, she knew that it would be impossible. He kept a tight reign. Undoubtedly, they belonged to each other, both brought up in perilous times, stringent, austere times, abuse not an arm's length away. Between them they had seen enough uncertainty. They too, had seen the humans.

Until her impending cloud lifted, she found it difficult to be giving, all the time aware of the uncertainty and in her heart knowing that her behaviour was missing its warmth and sincerity. On the strength that he said that he loved her and that he had always loved her and would continue to love her, she took an almighty chance. There was no easy way to say it. Probing ever so gently so as not cause alarm and dam the flow of words she asked him why compared to a year ago he was such a changed person. She wanted him to heal her still raw and gaping wounds of a year ago, to admit that had been the cause of her desperate unhappiness. She had lost her way. On Friday it was overcast and it rained. Surfacing from sleep her husband's grim mood set the tone for the day. The house felt too small. The overbearing tension was squeezing her against the walls. She fretted. Restless, she could settle to nothing. In the afternoon, she took her umbrella and went out in the rain. On Sunday they were having a cup of tea in the garden. So many times she had composed her words, got them ready to say, transferring them to the tip of her tongue then swallowed them whole, for her digestive system to regurgitate another time when all-of-a-sudden her husband said.

"It was a waste of a day on Friday. I should have gone out, gone to Bicester, made use of the day."

"It makes me feel really awful when there is such an atmosphere in the house."

"I'm not blaming you. It's not your fault. You haven't done anything wrong." Not comforted by that, she replied.

"Why is it, when you know how you are behaving, that you don't do something about it?"

"Are you a psychoanalyst or something?"

"No. It's just that when you are like that, it makes the house feel uncomfortable."

"You were all chirpy. You'll be sad." And with that he changed the subject. His mind was somewhere else. From the table, he was watching the fish in the pond.

LORDS

Understanding cricket would take a lifetime and she went with her husband not only to try and learn but also to enjoy the relaxing, easy atmosphere that surrounded the mysterious game. The backdrop was Lords. The warp and weft of the woven outfield had been cut with precision, the worn and yellowing tidy wicket was manicured and neatly rolled and brushed with a besom broom. The morning got off to a good start for the opposition. The thin crowd were fresh and paying attention. By 11.30 a.m. cans had been opened, champagne drunk from bright pink plastic flutes and coffee carefully carried. Besides watching the match, people were reading newspapers, wrestling with the pages in the puffing wind, that stopped and started intermittently, reading books, reading the Playfair Cricket Annual, the essential little book of cricket facts, thumbed at intervals as an unknown player appears or a bowling or batting achievement is in sight, and reading the score card, marking it when the need arose. They were eating and applying the sun cream. One, forgetting that he was in public, was picking his nose. Two rows down, but across the gangway, two weathered friends sat in identical colours and talked and talked and talked, now and then looking up to see what was happening. Slowly the sun made its way across the white tip-up seats, and jumpers were peeled off and sun hats put on. A man near the front, already in the sun took off his shirt, exposing his already tanned skin and draped himself over several chairs, aligning himself to the sun for an even bake and to maximise his potential of becoming even browner. Sitting slightly skew-whiff on his seat allowed him to take in the crowd, he was keen to see if they were admiring his physique and every now and then he stood to do some limbering stretches. The tantalizing sun was hiding behind the Media Centre and did not reach her. At 12.20 p.m. when she nearly thought it would, as it was one seat away, a great funnel of high cloud swept in changing the sky to an ominous grey.

They had moved several times, eventually sitting two rows in front of them. She assumed them to be father and son as they had nothing much to say to each other and although the father's was grey and the son covered his with a brown leather Stetson, they had the same thin, lank hair. From his weight and size it was hard to estimate the son's age. Maybe he was sixteen, but he could have been twelve. The son was nothing more than a big fat bespectacled boy, who bit his nails to the quick, probably coddled and pampered by an overprotective mother, sent out for the day with her husband so that she could have respite from their constant demands. The boy looked exactly like a bigger version of a boy that she knew who had got stuck in a loft hatch. Huffing and puffing he had managed to get into the loft to play with the extensive electric train-set that ran around the rafters, but just could not get his great wide girth out again. She sees him now, no longer a boy, stooped and oafish, waiting at the bus stop or in the supermarket on Saturday morning pushing the trolley for his mother, he too wore glasses on his big doughy face, the spongy jowls of his extra face, hanging where his neck should be, wearing beige and neutrals against his pasty skin he looked old fashioned and unhealthy, looking older than her husband sitting beside her. By now, he would be twenty-eight. The now persistent wind in the lofty heights of the Compton stand was cool. The father of the boy sat hunched against the cold, his hands were pressed together and gripped between his knees for warmth. Beside his son's broad fat shoulders, his punishing thinness shivered beneath his eau-de-nil shirt.

Into the afternoon the crowd began to suffer. The match had gone off the boil, lethargy and the effects of alcohol had kicked in, bodies slumped lower into seats, heads nodded and sleep ensued. At 212 runs, the spell was broken and a cheer from the crowd brought a dozing woman back to life, briefly participating before she reached down to retrieve her glass of champagne again and took another gulp, only to resume her siesta. On the field there was much huddling and cuddling. The mysteries of cricket.

"That'll be a five." She heard him thinking aloud and surfaced from the drowsiness of reading. A five. In all the hours of cricket she had listened to or watched she had never heard mention of a five. Her husband explained how a five could come about. "If the ball hit a helmet or a hat or a jumper left on the pitch, for whatever reason, it was a five. There was so much to learn about cricket.

It was the first time that she had shown her husband a piece of her writing. Carefully she selected two pieces that amounted to three pages of A4 paper. His initial reaction was to sigh, but took them from her anyway, one eye on the test match on the television. Straightaway he noticed a mistake. In a frenzy to get it down, she had carelessly missed an 'e' off a 'the'. Instantly jumping to conclusions, she knew he was going to find fault and wished that the words had stayed confined to the secret storage of the hard drive. Feeling hurt she waited quietly for the barrage of criticism that was sure to follow. She studied his reactions closely, waiting for the contours of his face to change, watching for an undulation in his expression, a hint of agreement on the corners of his mouth and creases to deepen and darken with satisfaction.

Not usually generous with compliments, they had to be earned, he showed his approval when a slow wide smile spread across his face and a chuckle of amusement escaped from his throat confirming his appreciation. Her heart lurched with pleasure. It was the ultimate compliment.

Sharing these private thoughts with her husband along with the majesty of the kite and the recent visit to Lords were times to cherish. His tone was less hostile and more relaxed and she felt more included. She saw a different man, affectionate and sensitive, alert to her feelings. Every now and then, in little measured doses he supplied bits of information, snippets that had surfaced in his mind and wanted to share with her. She smiled more often. Recently, these rare times had become less and less frequent. Back in April she had felt quietly encouraged that he was the one to instigate the wallpapering and had wanted her to help him.

HOUSEWORK HOLIDAY

They hadn't booked a holiday. To her it was often the cause of unnecessary stress and that she decided, she could do without. For once she was perfectly happy to drift along with whatever turned up and if nothing did, which was never the case, she was happy with that too. And so the long Utopian holidays, envied by some and grudged by others but so yearned for by her, stretched out as far as she could see. She wanted to feel that ordinary, 'stay at home days' were as good as any spent abroad. The 'ordinary', was so easily lost in the unfamiliar foreignness. She wanted to learn to love again without the distraction of the warm intoxicating seas, without the hindering language of flavours, all around, the culture different, speech confined for two weeks, to themselves. No. For once she did not crave the distance of far-away places. She had chosen to spend the holiday in this disjointed way, and her husband had not insisted on going away. Apart from trying to speak to her husband about her sorrow, she had no plans. If she succeeded, then her time had been well spent. She did not succeed.

Asking her now on the telephone, how she was spending her holiday, was like asking her son how he spent his day. Nothing sprung to mind "Doing this and that." She replied. Knowing how much she enjoyed going to places and doing things she could tell that her son was disappointed. He did not see his mother spending her day, doing jobs around the house. Not saying that she wouldn't do them, but she would do them before she went out and wouldn't even mention the fact that she had. In her heart she felt that he knew that something was bothering her. She tried to dispel any fears that he had, to assure him, saying nothing of her perpetual anguish, not wanting her lack of adventure construed as self-pity, convincing herself that this was what she had wanted.

All she had wanted was to see if she could trust herself to the ordinary domesticity around her, to see if she could cope with routine, the daily dull repetition, to practice for her pending retirement, when she and her husband would be together nearly all the time. She observed how he went about his day, what he did and when he did it, routines that had never mattered till now. In the busyness of life she had not paid attention. In between, there were distractions and they more than kept her busy and engrossed. She did not feel regret or disappointment. On the contrary, she had made, she thought, considerable progress and thus good use of her time. The installation of the new ironing board cover had restored the incentive to iron, and she no longer needed to pick the burnt foam backing of the old cover from the laundry. Out with the old and in with the new startling red mop activating her into mopping the kitchen floor. She hung the new curtains and bought extra hooks to improve the drape. There was just no way that the bay window could be seen to be attractive and considering its awkward shape, she had made it as good as she possibly could. She stripped the kitchen dresser and cleaned the glass knobs with vinegar and a toothbrush, an exacting, tiresome little job but rewarding seeing them sparkle once again. The new carpets were vacuumed, the loose wool fibres filling the dust bag far too quickly. She de-scaled the kettle and refreshed the plugholes. She wood-washed the cupboard doors and the kitchen chairs. Without the layer of dirt, the kitchen echoed. She wrote. She read. She drowsed. She filed and she shredded. Occasionally she went out. Being absorbed removed the constant nagging in her mind and although she had busied herself for the entire time with practicalities, she doubted that there would be the same enthusiasm, nor maintain her newly acquired domestic prowess in the long dark winter months and also, the house would be cold and while she had made a reasonable success of the 'holiday' she could not decide if being at home every day, was right for her.

It had taken a long time and a lot of courage to book the lessons and found excuses on several occasions to avoid the challenge. People said, "What do you need lessons for, you can swim?" And yes, she could, up to a point but she had been self-taught and knew that by being taught the correct technique, her stroke would improve and her confidence increase further, remembering a time when she wouldn't go out of her depth and nor would she put her face under the water. The next round of 'improvers' commenced on Thursday. How she floundered and thrashed about in the turbulence of nothing short of a washing machine on the rinse cycle, breathing in all the wrong places, gulping water, coughing and spluttering, stopping, gasping for breath and squeezing her nose. The teacher, Ian, started with the front crawl. Not knowing how to, it was the very stroke that she never used. He demonstrated straight legs that moved from the hip and for the arms 'along the thigh, elbows high, across the eye'. Feeling instantly disadvantaged, she lunged and flailed wildly. However, she was exhilarated by her defeat and would practice. Leaving her legs to trail along, she concentrated on her breathing. Fundamental. In a cordoned area of the pool she could overhear John, the swimming instructor saying to his pupil. "How is your maths? Can you count to three?" The little boy nodded. One, two, three, breath. One, two, three, breath. And so she rolled and tumbled up and down the length of the pool, determined and having the confidence already by not worrying about what people thought. One mother helping her daughter said to her, "You go".

"No" she puffed as she reached the end of the length. "You go".

"She's only practising". Only. What was only about practising?

"So am I". She replied, regaining her breath.

Before her next lesson she practised three times. How her shoulder's ached but she did not give in and even when her lessons came to an end, she continued to practice. A year later she could swim several lengths.

She had inherited her headstrong determination from her mother and attributed her impulsive remarkable energy to her consultant, who three times had negotiated the insidious shwannoma growing along her spinal cord, cutting it away as near as he dare to the nerves that allowed her to be able to walk. More than anything in the whole wide world, she wanted to walk. "I must be able to walk." It was imperative. And so each time after the long invasive surgery and still thick with anaesthetic, anchored to the bed with saline drips and blood drips and catheters and drains and wires, all linked to the many monitors, the first thing she did was to wriggle her toes. Until the first operation she had spent five years in chronic pain, pain that she could not begin to describe, searing, electrical, piercing spasms of pain, ripping through her body, draining her of her resources. Pain required great energy and she had none left. Sometimes she was convinced that she was dying a slow drawn out painful death and surely it was preferable, to the horrific nightmare taking-over and ruling her life. On bended knees they prayed for her. Ambulances came to the house and she was delivered screaming, as though deranged, covered in a blanket and fastened with a strap, to hospital wards, in waiting rooms when the pain was beyond control, everyone turned to look. At the time, her whole life became governed by appointments and the caustic effects of narcotics and hallucinogenic drugs administered to relieve the pain. Initially, not being believed added to the burden, trying to convince the medical profession of her vivid pain was a struggle in itself. The surgery left its mark. Every day it was there. Each time she took a step the numbness was a reminder. And, she had been robbed of desire. But she fought back. She was alive and she was walking, until the next time and she knew that there would be a next time, when her surgeon's careful, dedicated hands drew the scalpel once again along the length of her back and lifted the skin from her bones. While she had always worked tirelessly, her momentum increased, valuing every single moment of living, not one single second was taken for granted, not one single second was squandered. The energy, combined with the determination of a wildebeest, provided the recipe for her total passion for life. Optimistic, positive, hopeful, she had the wind in her sails and often took a dim view of people who did not aspire to her way of thinking, people who procrastinated or lacked vim or plainly couldn't be bothered. She was a 'can do' person.

AUGUST

Olney was all the richer for her spending £10 on her sister's sparkly bracelet, random coloured resin stones and silver coloured flowers, threaded with elastic, all the fashion at the moment, prettily wrapped in its own little carrier bag and tied with a ribbon. Now all that was needed was one of those second-hand puffy packets that had accumulated in the kitchen drawer, just waiting for such an occasion.

Walking into Olney in the dripping wet afternoon, in search of a mirror to hang above the fireplace, it occurred to her that there was a glaring error, an unforgivable mistake in her manuscript and it had already been posted. She had been proofreading her book, which, she didn't think that she did very well, tending to skip over words and read them without thinking. As she walked, she remembered Burgess's where she bought her bike and where they supplied the Calor Gas for the heater in her workroom. Oh my God. In her book she had called the big agricultural shop the wrong name. Reaching for the local books on the bookshelf, she found a picture of Cooper's. How could she have made such an obvious mistake? It was Cooper's, not Burgess's. Without delay, she sent the production team an email to rectify the error. Besides the millions of commas and hyphens, colons and semi-colons and some spelling mistakes that had been checked, there was a word that needed confirmation, a word that had been suggested but could not be found in any of her ancient, but usually adequate dictionaries. It was' poseur', and meant 'a person who behaves affectedly in order to impress others'. And just while she was in the library checking the word, she happened to see a book by John Clark called *The Tories*. She needed to change her 'Torries' to 'Tories'. She sent another email to clarify the two words. One mistake, not grammatical, remained. It sat comfortably on the page.

For a morsel of a minute there were no voices to be heard, no people to be seen and no traffic on the move. It felt like France. Still and quiet. The warm balmy air hung thickly, trapped in the street between the houses. A deep, velvet warmth emitting from the earthy brick Victorian walls breathed on her bare arms, as she walked into town. Almost by mistake, as though it was trying to avoid its own destiny, a dry leaf, a juvenile, only months old scampered giddily in tinkling circles, to be silenced abruptly in the gutter. Then nothing moved. Above, ragged clouds in the high summer sky smudged and faded to vanish in the distance. Nearby, the trees, a gauzy vapour of green, sighed. But in the street, for that brief moment in time, it felt like France.

Feeling buoyant she wrote again to 'Woman's Hour' and enclosed another copy of her book. The fiction producer might just say. "Oh, for God's sake, not this again." Stuffing it in her bag to read on the way home. She liked to think that she would read it from its lovely patchwork front cover to the bar code on the back, not just flick through. And it would leave her feeling, well she didn't know how it would leave her feeling. Surprised? Impressed? Why should it surprise her? The wealth of talent all around goes unseen by most. People do not exploit their hidden talents. At school she sees the most outstanding talent every day, artwork adorning the walls, quite priceless, as good as anything anywhere, but not recognized as such. She was not so surprised. The paintings were energetic and vibrant, new and fresh. Painted within the constraints of the limited school budget and without experience, here and there in the week, between other lessons, after PE, feeling hot and sweaty or freezing cold, before lunch, when the pangs of hunger overtake anything. It was a challenge for many and each rose to the occasion in their way. Some very unlikely characters produced brilliant work and that to her, made it all the more amazing. Keeping some on a chair long enough was in itself amazing, as was holding a pencil or a brush. They did these works of art without the props that adults claim to need, without the stimulation of alcohol, or drugs or caffeine. They did it on the strength of a bowl of 'Rice Krispies' or nothing at all or if it was the afternoon, a few sweets or a bag of crisps, nothing sustaining. With encouragement from their teacher, they had to do it there and then, no shirking, or putting-off, called, work avoidance in school. "Are you going to make a start then?" How could anyone make a start? And how do you start? (She must remember to be more forgiving). After the age of 14, the artists might never paint a still-life again, they might never sketch their friend in charcoal ever again. Just think of the wasted talent. Since that day in the school hall when she sat the 11 and wrote nothing but her name, it had taken a lifetime to pick up a pen and write. Even then, she had been frightened of failing, of not coming up to the mark, of letting her mother down. She felt that unless her book was read by someone who could put it on the map, how could potential readers know it was there to be found? She also sent thirteen letters to different branches of Waterstones, requesting that they stocked her book. All it needed was a little bit of luck. Good luck. It deserved a chance. It stood a chance. Privately, she hoped that it would get off the ground, before the next one was published and was guilty from time to time of buying all the papers again, unable to resist checking the book reviews, just to see if she was mentioned. Sometimes misgivings threatened. She was not arrogant or conceited, nor boastful. Being modest and quite happy to be anonymous she found difficulty convincing people to buy it and read it. It was not as though she had not already carved a name for herself. Many of her designs had been in newspapers and magazines in the early 70s. At the time she had thought nothing of it. She didn't punch the air or go in for high fives or even rush out and buy a copy. It was her job and she took the success in her stride, not mentioning it at all unless it came into conversation. Somehow this was unexpected.

Hanging on to summer, she went to London in a dress, her legs bare, tinted with the faint sun-kissed look out of a bottle and her high heeled espadrilles. Totally impractical, she knew that. Whenever she wore the dress she wanted to jive, but jiving had been before her time and she didn't know how to. There was a train at five past, and although not in a hurry, the queue for tickets seemed as slow as a snail. Suddenly the pressure to get on that particular train was imperative. Her impatience consumed her beyond reason. She could hear the couple in front of her saying that too. Agitated, moving to and fro, they didn't think they would make it either and were looking at alternative times and all the combinations of factors that each time presented. Why was buying a ticket so stressful? Suddenly, the queue slipped to nothing in moments, then, as she was walking down the stairs she could see that there was a tempting train that went to Clapham Junction waiting to leave at sixteen minutes past, totally empty, on platform two, the pull towards it was great, but instead she joined the throng on platform one. In the end, it would be quicker and would arrive in Euston by eleven. Now the next little hurdle, because she would be in London earlier than expected, was there enough time to get to the Thames Barrier and get back to Imperial College for one, where she was meeting her son for the all-important lunch? Decisions. Decisions. Although she felt good in the dress, it was not suitable. Going down the escalator a great parachute of flowery cotton chintz blew up around her when a funnel of wind got underneath. Walking along, she was aware that any circulation of air might lift it. Catching the Northern line to Bank, she made her way to Greenwich on the DLR, then asked, what looked like a local, the directions to the Thames Barrier. "Take the 177 bus. You'll catch it across the road there." He said, pointing. Thanking him, she crossed the road and waited no more than a moment. Crossing continents the bus trundled along and she realized that maybe she wouldn't be in South Kensington for one after all and searched in the little zipped pocket in her bag for the important telephone numbers, written down on the smallest piece of paper and carried everywhere, in case needed. God, she had cleared it out along with her Tesco card and her library card and other superfluous odds-and-ends. Unlike some people who could remember telephone numbers, she did not have the storage capacity. She only remembered her own and there was no-one at home to relay a message. Not being able to phone her son and explain that she would be late dampened her visit to the Barrier. Once off the bus, she asked directions again and took the path. Although she felt rushed, it was impressive, she had always wanted to see it and now she had, taking some picture to capture the engineering feat. As it does sometimes, going back seemed quicker. Her son had nearly given-up. Lunch was good, quick but good and after catching-up with the news, the driving lessons and the house hunting and the swimming lessons and the book, followed by a speedy return to work, they said their goodbyes. No longer in a desperate hurry, she popped into the V&A, to saunter around the ground floor, taking in the sinks of the Italian Renaissance, the Chinese kimonos, Raphael's cartoons and the Fashion gallery. She felt nothing but privileged to be able to walk in off the street into another time, another place, to stand back and admire what had been. Down the road, was her son intent on trying to find something waiting to be discovered and here were the things that had gone before. Catching the bus back to Euston she sat on the top-deck and devoured the metropolis, the endless ribbons of people on the crowded pavements or uncoiling from the underground, along Brompton Road, into Knightsbridge, then Hyde Park Corner and Piccadilly into Charing Cross Road and Tottenham Court Road. She never tired of the view. She never tired of living.

Embracing the bus was not usual, preferring instead the convenience of her car, but at the same time grudging the cost of parking and worse, coming back late and the car park in lurking darkness. She had long forgotten that feeling of waiting for the bus, the element of risk that could change the shape of the day if it did not come on time, anxiously busying herself, reading the timetable, checking her watch, searching her purse for £2 and holding it tightly, enduring the grimacing stares of passing drivers or their passengers and looking and waiting all the time for a glimpse of the faithful stubby turquoise vehicle that would transport her to where she needed to go, all the time listening for the drone as it changed gear and slowed to turn right at the roundabout and the relief that she felt when it appeared, stepping up and slipping her two neat pounds into the worn shallow saucer below the glass partition. "To the station, please." Tearing the ticket from the machine she thanked the driver and retrieved her 5p change. All the tension of waiting evaporated. The bus allowed a different freedom. Being that bit higher, she could look out of the window at passing traffic, and the trees, which she loved and sometimes the gardens hidden behind them. She watched the people getting on and off the bus. She heard the sharp ping of the bell. She really must get round to getting some new glasses, she thought the poster said the 'mobile bonking service ...' As the bus neared the station, it joined with two others and in a pack of three they chased around, accelerating together, swinging round roundabouts together, pulling up together on the finishing line for their drivers' break.

Coming home, after two buses had passed her by, she realised that she was waiting at the wrong stop, assuming that the stop she was dropped off at in the morning was the one for the return journey. She walked the few steps to the right stop. A sudden torrential downpour had everyone running for shelter. Even though it said that number one buses went from that stop, she wanted confirmation and asked the lady to her right. Yes it was, and for a moment went into the intricate network of the buses, which before this day she had no need to know. Even before she spoke, she knew she had something urgent to say, something much more urgent than the buses. Without prompting she came straight out with it. "I'm a great grandmother. She was born this morning at half past eight." She had had the call the previous evening and had lain awake all night waiting. Understandably, she felt tired, but was obviously bursting with pleasure, wanting to share her good news, elation written all over her warm open face. Both stepped into the rain and onto the bus and continued to chat sitting one behind the other. Unable to drive, she used the buses frequently and warned of the many disadvantages. If she had not taken the bus she would not have met this dear person and felt sure that they would meet again, probably on the number one bus.

Before leaving in the morning, she had left a note on the table. Written on the back of a printed out map of Worcester were the easy-to-follow instructions. It was all ready to go.
Dinner is easy.
Tip rice into colander and bring to boiling, no. 4 until red-hot.
Tip curry into pan (in small bowl in fridge) heat gently and thoroughly no. 3ish.
Stir occasionally, maybe add a little water.
It must be piping hot.
Voila.

The pans and the colander were left ready on the cooker along with the wooden spoon, the water in the big pan for steaming the rice and the dinner itself, planned for re-using from the previous day, was covered and in the fridge. On her return, her eyes went straight away to where she had left the note. It had gone. In their house notes can be around for years and yet this note had gone.

She had finished her book, all five hundred and fifty one pages, picked up and put down countless times and renewed from the library at least four times. It had been a good story, in her mind, not an unfamiliar one. It worried her that Melvin Bragg used a great many adjectives, like the ones she used in her writing, to describe the love and deep emotional upheaval between Joe and Natasha. He also used words that she had never seen before, literary words, not to be found in her mini-dictionary but sure to be found in the dictionary in the library. Being so clever, he probably didn't refer to a dictionary, he, she was sure was a thesaurus of words, stored alphabetically in his head, never needing to consult a dictionary, unlike her, who was always thumbing through, looking for good words or checking a spelling. While there were numerous dictionaries on the bookshelf she did not own a thesaurus or had ever used one until she randomly, taking the register one morning in an English classroom, picked one up to browse through, waiting for the big hand to reach 8. 50 a.m. Imagine her surprise when she read all the alternatives for a word, removing all the hard work out of searching 'manually', so while, again randomly wasting time in Oxfam one Saturday morning, trying to resist the tempting offers, she came across a thesaurus for £5, it had been £20 and its condition was immaculate. How could someone simply throw it out? Of course she could have taken advantage of the thesaurus on the 'tools' bar, but one click too many or in the wrong spot could render her work lost to the mystery of the computer.

PUNISHMENT

They sat without speaking. Everything that she had rehearsed and intended to say, she failed to say, instead she was silent. It was quite simply impossible to say what she wanted to say, to say what she was really thinking, without hurting.

"Sticks and stones may break your bones,
But names will never hurt you."

She didn't ever remember being slapped or hit with a stick or a strap as a child. Her abuse was subtle. Initially it went unseen to the naked eye, leaving no trace. But it was there, if anyone cared to look. For her, it was impossible to erase the indelible stain, woven into the fabric of her life. Over the years, the memories had dimmed, but living with the pain and the shame had never quite gone away. She said, right from the beginning that if he ever hit her, she would leave. It was 'normal' in those days for wives and children to be beaten. Both she and her husband had grown up with it, avoiding the opportunity at all costs. Their fathers had high opinions of themselves, they were domineering and controlling. Administrating physical punishment along with persistent humiliation made their fathers feel powerfully important and that being the head of the family, it was to be expected. Now, in their thirties when alcohol had loosened their tongues her children were surprised to learn how their friends also suffered at the punishing hands of their fathers. As she knew they would, they remembered feeling the thud of a Church's leather slipper brought down on their duvets when there was too much hilarity at bedtime. No amount of wriggling could escape the thwack of the slipper. Their father would remove a slipper then holding it in his right hand, charge up the stairs two at a time and attack the bed covers until shadows stole into the room and silence settled. Behind the curtain, the full moon bleeds and with every thump wielded, so does she. While the duvet cushioned the blows leaving no red welts or inflamed skin, they would never forget the determined hate in his eyes and the cruel anger in his voice when he lifted the slipper to full stretch. He was as much a bully as his own father. The awfulness was that she too was complicit, an accomplice, knowing full well the damage it was causing, feeling racked with guilt and overcome with shame each time that he brought the slipper down. Her protests went unheard. She was powerless. Just the thought of anyone harming her children filled her with fear. Her husband never hit her. She gave him no reason. Instead, over time there were underlying demands, which he hoped she would deliver and if she didn't, she got the numbing silence treatment. It might have been nothing more than a difference of opinion, or a genuine mistake. She wanted to say that silences did hurt. And hurt more deeply, than he could ever imagine. Bruises eventually faded, inflicted wounds healed but she nursed the silences forever. How she needed to speak-up and clear the air around her, but he seemed so uncomplicated, sitting there, fishing, singing and whistling a medley of tunes, one dissolving into another. He had a good voice. How could she disturb the innocence and spoil the comfortable aura that drifted in the current around them, based on such flimsy reasons? How could she abandon him to a sleepless night of tossing and turning, spoiling his contentment and physical ease when the quiet darkness around him, wanted to gather him into her arms? How could she journey by his side, lightly exchanging words, him, listening to her and trying to master the rasping voice of Tom Waits, then abruptly change the subject, for him to withdraw from conversation altogether and dissolve into unhappiness? How could she spoil the ambience and easy rapport over breakfast in the garden, dappled light, birds singing, Sunday morning sounds, the smell of bacon? How could she? At the same time, how could he not see that there was something eroding away at her mind, distracting and worrying her? How could he be so unaware and yet at the same time so sensitive to his own troubled scars that refused to heal?

Bound by their love, she knew that in time she would need him and she knew also that he would need her.

They lay side-by-side in the dark. Her eyes were wide open and out of nowhere, she suddenly heard her voice. "How is it that you are so much nicer to be with, compared with this time last year? Do you know?" She continued. "I wanted to leave you."

"Where would you go?" He did not seem to be shocked.

"I don't know. I would work it out."

As far as he could see, he had nothing to justify, nothing to apologise for. He refused to be drawn into something he might regret. Sometimes, she thought he knew how desperate she felt, as though he read her mind. But he never said. He would come close and hold her in his arms, comforting.

Her son arrived, without warning, to take her to where the Land Rover was being repaired. This was not, not normal. Yesterday he had arrived without warning and had a lunch of the best part of a French stick, three sausages, onions and tomato sauce, which until he walked through the door she had no idea she was making. Quickly she changed, in other words she rolled her trousers down and applied some lipstick. On top of her top she wore the most recently acquired, summery, vaguely striped cotton/linen jacket that creased on demand. She locked the house and climbed into the blue van. They went the usual way to the village where she had grown up. They were going to Poplar Farm to see Dave, a good sound name for someone who deals with motor repairs. Joe, her son pulled in off Castle Hill Road. Dave had been dying to ask about the surname on the invoice, but knowing the village as well as she did, she was the first to speak. "Do you come from here?" He replied that he came from Dunstable, but that his wife did. And so he asked about the surname and it transpired that all three seemed to have an inner knowledge of each other, in a round-about sort of way. And then, in the massive barn next to where they were standing, there was a man dressed from head to foot in protective clothing, standing in a cherry-picker perched above the tractor, systematically moving along the wall with a chemical sprayer, fumigating the walls, scrolling up and down, up and down, the fine spray turning them the colour of cement, she assumed, to remove any traces of bacteria, getting it ready for the cows to come back in for the winter. The man driving the tractor was called Tim, she remembered Tim, a year older than her. She remembered his sister Julie, two years younger. In the whir of the moment and she could not recollect how, but checking that it was safe to enter, she was suddenly in the darkness of the barn, skipping through the great shell of space towards Tim on the far side. In a sudden burst, glimpses of a another time appeared before both of them, how the farm used to be, the animals, his parents, her parents, school, Mrs Jones, village life, everything that had gone before crammed into the four corners of the empty barn "Do you know who I am?" she said as she approached, aware of him scrutinizing her in the dimness. "You're a Weir."

"I am. I am Louise Anne. I remember you and how is Julie?" She asked.

"She's just walked the dogs. She lives in Hockliffe."

She remembered his face but rotund was the best way to describe Tim.

They talked about the Land Rover because that is what made the chance encounter happen. It never ceased to amaze her that while something was happening it was a real job to take it all in and an even greater job to recollect it later. She said that she had bought the Land Rover for her husband's birthday a year ago and that it was in a poor sad state and badly needed a make-over to pass its MOT. Fishing was mentioned and he went on to talk about Brown's in Leighton Buzzard and yes she knew of the place, off the by-pass that now apparently sold more fishing tackle than tractors. Well it wasn't every day that you needed a tractor. The man in the chemical suit reappeared. Had he actually gone? Had he been waiting, suspended in the basket to be moved further along the wall and in the rush of introductions, she had not noticed. She couldn't be sure, but he seemed anxious to get on, so they said goodbye. Out in the sunshine again, they stood admiring the gleaming chassis for the Land Rover, securely padlocked to the fence. Dave said that he would be in touch. Joe turned the van around and they went home the way they had come. By four o'clock, the sunny racing sky was replaced with darkening cloud. Rain seemed imminent but she continued to sit, bare armed, in the swirling wind.

On the weather map a swathe of blue, stippled with white dashes across the southern half of England, indicated that summer had come to sudden end and she found herself reaching for warm cardigans.

BANGOR

It was the start of term, the time of year when she remembered moving to Bangor, albeit temporarily, recalling the late September warmth, walking along the pier, beachcombing for exhibits for the nature table, a feather or a shell, the refectory, taking a tray and sliding it along the serving rail, selecting this and that and sitting with her 'new' friends to eat, the accommodation on the very steep hill shared with other students, playing hockey and seeing the grandeur of the university opposite. The memories of her short time at St. Mary's were rich and lasting. They parked in the long-stay near the harbour and walked. After the ambient temperature of the car for four hours the air snapped in the cold brisk wind. The narrow high street had been block paved but unlike Luton, it was thriving and bustling with students and people out shopping on Saturday afternoon. Her husband was searching his memory, trying to picture himself leaving to drive the 200 miles home without her. They turned left, leading from the high street and started to climb. The road narrowed. After forty-two years she was not sure and he doubted too, that it was the right road. Making enquiries with a woman leaving her house, they were assured that it was. He forged ahead, walking far too quickly, his tenacity as bad as it was in Amalfi when he climbed the most ridiculous path at such a pace that he collapsed on the bed, rivulets of sweat pouring down his neck, his hair was pasted to his forehead, his pulse was racing, his red face was a sheen of moisture, his veins distended from over-exertion, he was gasping for breath, totally exhausted. He wouldn't be told. Sadly, the building was in a terrible state of disrepair and that the college itself had been relocated and become part of the university. Her husband took some photos of her, beside the post box where she would have posted her love letters to him, the college in the background. She took a picture of the house that she shared with others on the very steep hill. It was shuttered and neglected, its paintwork peeling, weeds encroaching, shopping trolleys pushed into the corner. Pushing a trolley on a glossy interior surface was bad enough, how could anyone push one up the hill? Apart from the textbooks, bought for the course, she had nothing from those days all those years ago. It was hard remembering and separating from her memory visits to the city years before with her sister and parents. Into her mind came the painful image of her mother, her mouth drawn, complaining bitterly about a café in the high street that her husband had taken the three of them into. It was not to her mother's liking, it was more like a rough transport café, a greasy spoon of a place, a dump, with a yellowing ceiling and smeary windows, a damp smoky haze pervaded and clung to the surfaces in the mean crowded space and the melamine tables were littered with sauce bottles and ashtrays and chipped cups. Her mother much preferred the elegance of a traditional tearoom and felt awkward and embarrassed and would gladly have paid more to sit in pleasant surroundings with her daughters, especially on holiday, while her husband on the other hand had little appreciation for her genteel ways and thought her excesses a waste of money. With all the time in the world, he sat and smoked and sipped at his scalding tea, while she grimaced and tried to fill the air with small talk, all the time trying to cover-up her anger. Immediately she sensed an atmosphere between her parents and couldn't bear the bad feeling that the altercation caused. Living on top of each other in a ridge tent, there was no escape. Leaving her thoughts, she and her husband took the sign for the pier and paid the nominal 25p each to stroll its length towards Anglesey. It was not how she remembered it, and wondered why a different pier came into her imagination, finding it disconcerting having her thoughts rearranged. On the left, in the distance was one of the bridges. In the sunlight everywhere was clean and orderly. The white washed cottages snuggled on the shore and to the tourist, it was a romantic picture postcard view, a desirable residence. The sun reflected off the windows on the houses dotted around on the island. Everything sparkled. Below the broad rain-washed boards, the sea puckered into layers of shining slate. Gulls swooped and dived. Against the blue, a flock of oystercatchers cried, driven on the wind to land some way off. Out of the wind the sun bathed their faces. Turning round at the end of the pier, they could see in the distance the sprouting peaks of the Snowdonia National Park.

SEPTEMBER

The postman had left a card saying that there was a package awaiting collection. It was from the publishers. Waiting until she got to school she took the scissors and carefully opened the envelope. It was so exciting and she could see that it was to be published shortly. It was the final proof for reading, checking and approving. Within days another letter arrived requesting her to do a written author's interview about her writing and her book, could she also record the interview. Horror of horrors, instantly remembering her nerve-racking radio experience earlier in the year, she set-to. Not being a 'media professional' it was flawed with fear and took several attempts before it was done. She was modest and found it was difficult to wax-lyrical about her achievements, agreeing that there was much room for criticism and sent a letter along with the CD explaining its failing and that she would do it again if need be.

The optician, only the other day asked if she had headaches and she had said thankfully not. Over the years migraines had lessened and lessened, so surfacing at 3 a.m. on Saturday morning with a grinding pain that seemed to move about her head depending on how she lay on the pillow, threw her into a state of anxiety, knowing full well how her precious day would pan out. Immediately, she blamed the red wine, drunk too quickly and the fact that she had not eaten anything very much, preferring instead sun-dried tomatoes laced with acidity regulator and nuts with lashings of salt and camembert and smoked ham, tasty little morsels of this and that, instantly gratifying, bought along with the shopping on the way home, and the fact that for two nights during the week, she had not slept well. Any one could have contributed to her fragile state. Getting up, she went downstairs for a glass of water and two paracetamols, returning to bed, only to toss and turn and doze and try to shake off the wretched feeling. By eight, she gallantly got up, hung out the washing, had a shower and made some tea, then half in her jeans and half in her dressing gown she crawled back into bed and pulled the covers around her. All day she drifted in and out of consciousness. Dreams and thoughts interrupted the pain. With her senses heightened, the traffic seemed incessant, nothing short of the third runway, a stone's throw away. One car after another streamed up and down the road taking off for the place over there. Where was it all going? Where had it come from? By the afternoon the morning busyness in the town had dissolved and still she was alert to the departure and arrival of cars. In her mind she tried to work it out. There had to be a solution and she proceeded to plan how to divert the traffic away from her road. Drifting into a shallow sleep she was immersed in a cloud of indefinable dense grey particles and then on waking she could see floaters, a semi-quaver and a quaver gravitated to the left then to the right beneath her eyelid. Between her ear and the pillow there was an open cast mine and she was aware of the low-geared growl of a lorry full of stone, hauling itself up a long slow incline. Her head was heavy, her mouth was dry and she wanted water, her glass was beside her but she had no energy to lift her head, she needed an extendable bendy straw. The curtains were closed against the harsh bright light of day. Lacking energy, she could barely speak, managing no more than one word acknowledgements. She was better to be left alone. Her bone coloured face was devoid of expression. Her friend used to claim that she looked more dead than alive. The weak desperate feeling had to be endured and she knew that it would eventually pass. And it did.

Even though it wasn't time, why should there be a time, they sat at Twiggies on the corner and ordered fish and chips and a beer, taking stock of their immediate surroundings, her husband in the shade, her in drenching sun. The vicinity was not to her liking. Much was English, a cross between a holiday camp and a fun fair and their bread and butter depended on the tasteless bars with oversized screens blaring out and supermarkets and tacky shops selling pink cuddly toys and cheap plastic trinkets and gaudy trash from China. Many shops and restaurants were already closed for the season. Se vende signs were everywhere, waiting for the current economic climate to turn around.

Apart from the roads and the fields, the whole of Spain seemed to be carpeted in a comprehensive range of tiles, terra-cotta, concrete, ceramic, glazed, resin, plastic, etc. The filthy pavements were tiled in various patterns and were in a various state of decay, many were uneven, broken like chipped teeth or had no kerb to support and so they fell away. Where they could, seeds blown on the wind, grew in the cracks into tufts of coarse weeds. Thin scurrying ants made their home in the land of tiles, relentlessly going to and fro. Where there had been an effort to lower kerbs to make them 'wheel-chair friendly' they were in places, so steep that able people tripped up. Chewing gum, casually spat and black with dirt stuck fast between the tiles. Mierda de perros too, in contact with a flip-flop spread itself, like paste in the grooves until it dried to dust in the heat. Wherever there was a wall, over the wall would be rubbish, dumped, even though beside the wall there was a fleet of recycling hoppers to fulfil every need. Spain.

On Sunday they walked, intent on finding the beach with

the all-important facilities, to discover nothing more than a cove, a narrow inlet, pretty enough but inadequate. Her disappointment was obvious. The few sun-chairs were occupied and there were no parasols. People sat themselves on their towels, or stretched out on the unwashed sand in the bleaching light, large people looking horribly uncomfortable, marooned like beached whales. Children played with their buckets and spades, their parents unable to relax for the discomfort, applying sun lotion liberally to their children and repositioning their hats and continually checking that they hadn't been stolen or drowned or just wondered off. Unlike the other tourists, making do with a bad job, trying to convince themselves that they were having a good time when all the time they were glum and reticent, she couldn't stay, refusing to sit at all and stood impatiently waiting to leave. As they left, other people heading for the beach looked hopeful, small children in tow, excited, skipping along, folded towels, buckets and spades hanging skewwhiff from pushchairs, full of fun and anticipation, the prospect of building a castle or catching a fish in the rock pools. Their pleasure would last the day but she doubted that their parents would last five minutes when they stepped onto the sand. There would be tears.

Walking back, they found a bar overlooking the sparkling sea and sat for hours over a long leisurely lunch, listening to the waves breaking over the rocks. The vino-tinto relaxed and the bean stew nourished, she let the sun pour over her and she was glad that the beach had failed to meet her expectations. Once eating, cats slunk in to sit patiently at their feet hoping for a morsel of food. The meow of a faded beige cat with milky eyes captured her attention along with the soft thud of a mouse. Loving the blissful warmth of the sun-baked tiles, he stretched out, playing with a mouse under a nearby chair, the tip of his tail twitching with satisfaction. It all seemed so normal.

In the night, the most horrendous wind got up, disturbing sleep and though not immediately next to the sea, she imagined great roaring waves washing over the complex and pulling back, like sea breaking over pebbles, washing around the sun chairs allowing them to float about. The gusting wind continued all day. The palms were turned inside out, twisting and writhing, their stout trunks holding fast. The palms struck up a symphony, their smooth shiny fronds gleamed with rain and as soon as it landed the raindrops were snatched away again in the wind. Driving rain dimpled the pool. The children's style was curtailed. A hardy, shapeless, pale skinned girl, with the look of a Celt, sporting a mass of red hair braved the elements. No shouts of laughter. Gulls allowed themselves to be carried about, sparrows rushed from bush to bush in groups of two or three. All day the wind pressed into corners and crevices, extractors and Spanish arches, crying and moaning, unable to escape and at three a storm broke, loud claps of thunder shook the apartment, lightening lit the still darkening sky. Rain fell in sheets eventually falling as hailstones as big as golf balls. She pulled a blanket, her only source of heat around her and slept in fits. This was not the picture in the glossy brochure. The sun coloured and made it come alive. Without it, it was as cold and as drab as England and she was not prepared. She was not fond of the shimmering tiled areas and the blue shaped pools advertised in brochures, she often found them to be misleading and in her opinion did not live up to her expectations. The brochure promised warmth and she had packed accordingly, flimsy cotton dresses in pale colours, sandals and two little cardigans just in case, no warmth, nothing remotely cosy. Thankfully, pyjamas went in the bag as an afterthought because there was space. They spent the day reading and drinking iron coloured tea that tasted thick and strange even though they had brought their "own" tea bags and used semi-skimmed milk, deciding that it must be the water. Eventually the sky brightened, the tiles dried and the swarthy Celt appeared again at the side of the pool.

They checked the bus times and went to Ciutadalla on the bus. There, in the dark of a doorway, she heard the slow swish of a broom on the tiles. Locals carried their sticks of bread. People sat under trees and spoke Spanish. This was Spain.

They walked around until one o'clock in the freezing wind but a brightening sky, looking like tourists with nothing better to do with their time, then boarded the bus again back to their resort, to be dropped off outside their favourite Spanish bar. They chose a table out of the wind and she sat with her back to the wall and the sun on her face and ate bean stew again and drank red wine, watching the swell rising and falling, listening to the heaving sea below thundering into the cliffs to explode over the rocks. Pressing into fissures, the spray leapt into the air to be carried over the edge of the land in the wind and returned to the sea in rivulets and gullies. Gulls stretched out, white against the sky, lifted and hung in the wind, their thin legs dangling. To be replaced with more, blousy clouds blustering through to vanish without trace. The winds brought dust from Africa. A thin layer of grit lay on everything. Waiters apologised as they wiped their tables in big sweeping 'S' shapes.

As a rule, they didn't buy a daily paper but while they were away, they bought the Daily Mail at a very inflated price and read the rubbish from cover to cover, listened to her husband selecting the winners at various meetings, which he was very good at, and did the crossword. An edible starch with four letters, the second letter is "A" her husband would say when he had exhausted his ideas. Well, it wasn't flour or potatoes or bread. "What about cake?" She said. The paper was like a comfort blanket and carried everywhere until it finally became an irritation and pushed into the carrier bag for recycling. So while lying on her back beside the pool, positioned to look her best, it came to her. "It's sago." She said. And of course with that, brought memories of school dinners and other milk puddings like semolina and tapioca and rice dished out with a ladle and served with a spoonful of red jam and the Melamine plates in faded shades, rose pink, primrose yellow, sky blue and apple green. Above her, in the plain blue sky the planes shone, their feint ruled lines of gold, joined the continents. Slowly the vapour trails dissolved and drifted into a fringe of tassels or a giant vertebrae or feathers or smudgy paws walking uncertainly across the sky.

She would have a go at Sudoko, the annoying little grids of numbers, but not for long, she found them exasperating and pointless unlike crosswords, which propelled thoughts in different directions. There was no room for manoeuvre with Sudoku and she hadn't got a rubber to erase the mistakes, of which, there were many. Then it looked a mess. She also read the newspaper and absorbed the health and diet advice, tore out a recipe for 'Little blueberry puddings with lemon curd sauce' and one for 'Sticky spiced lamb shanks'. Things that she had never thought about before, came to her attention, most of it was drivel.

It was undoubtedly the end of the season. It was like clearing the table when the guests were still eating. Rubbish bins were dismantled and piled in a shed, lamps were carefully covered and taped or removed completely, the white plastic sun beds were gradually removed until only a handful remained. The maintenance men jet washed round the pool. The menu lessened.

She tried to make herself think, to analyse why she was so against such a straightforward thing as making a cup of tea, eventually concluding that it was because by doing these things under duress she felt like her mother had felt, at her husband's beck and call. If he had been disabled or unwell she would have gladly co-operated. But he was not. She couldn't bear to see herself in this situation, plagued with resentment and instantly fired-up with anger, over something so trivial. Words retorted, left a sour taste in her mouth. Also, his authoritarian tone opened old wounds, wounds delivered by her father over fifty years ago, that had never been resolved, making her wary and on her guard against abuse. Only as she got older did she realise how damaged she had been. She had endured years of ridicule and crushing humiliation at the hands of her father and he had shown no remorse, he never did make an effort to make things right. Her worthless father had lived long after his expiry date and had never been punished. She had wanted retribution, but as a child or as a young person she would not have been listened to let alone believed. And how could she hurt her mother? As an adult, she threw herself into her new life, leaving the past temporarily behind her, until of course, her husband had a paddy and everything came flooding back. She did not want to feel beholden or indebted or made to sit on the naughty step or sent to Coventry for not conforming and towing the line, like a disobedient child, bullied until she obeyed. And when she did do what was expected, she didn't do it with love and this in itself made her feel as bad as not doing it. The starchy threat of these unpredictable outbursts was always there and it saddened her that she couldn't be herself. Her heart lurched at the outset of a confrontation, giving her no choice. Just thinking about it, her eyes brimmed with tears. Until he had asked for a cup of tea and she refused to make it, they had shared a good week away.

CARRIE

On their return, the news clouded the sun and tarnished the golden afternoon. She passed a perfectly good teaspoon, lying on the path. A man wearing a green T-shirt waited by his car for her to go by. Into her scarf she murmured thanks. All around golden snow lightly twirled to the ground, littering the path with coppery leaves, sycamore, lime and beech. Outside the Dolphin she saw a man having a cigarette and a beer, wearing a padded jacket exactly like her mother's, that she had given to the charity shop in the high street, it was good to see it being worn instead of gathering dust on the peg in the porch. "And how's the author?" She was glad to stop and talk, to share a brief literary conversation with Peter, who had much to say, but found it difficult to remember. What do you say to your son, when his love spirals to earth like the leaves around her? He didn't need to say. "Did you have a good holiday?" Already, it had been forgotten. It seemed unimportant. Now, motionless, standing beside him, there was nothing to say. "I'm so sorry." She said, wrapping her arms around him. Yet only a few hours earlier they had stood waiting for the bus to take them back to the airport, the pink morning reflected on the downy feathers of the gulls as they wheeled and called, their wings outstretched, their legs tucked neatly towards their tails. Really the holiday ended as they reached the big airy check-in with its hard cold surfaces, administration and legalities, then upstairs, waiting in departures, the brightness of shops, people and clatter. Dinner was a silent affair, her husband started to speak and found that he couldn't. He was not good with death. Afterwards he busied himself, moving the clocks back an hour, ready for the morning. They were joined in their sorrow. Fiercely written on the back of the note that she had left with love on the kitchen table before they left was the word 'RULES'.

He was broken hearted. No words could compensate. More than anything she wanted to comfort him, to protect him from the awfulness but could muster no words to make it better. Nothing she said could make it right, ever. The television was on in the corner, oblivious to the streaming commentary, of no consequence to her, she was aware of the green screen changing as different cameras honed in on the match. Minutes earlier her husband had been watching but had removed himself as his son was ready for a lift home. Although uninterested, she left it on for company. As soon as his father had left her eldest son appeared. Dropping heavily, he collapsed beside her in the gap between her and the arm of the settee. For hours they were immersed, pressed against each other, awkwardly folded in arms. Their hearts thumped faster and louder as they had before he was born. Their pulses raced. Aware of and sensitive to the distress in the sitting room when her husband returned, he decided to go straight to bed. The football finished and something else came on. Long painful silences interrupted the shuddering incoherent sobbing, the howling wails and the piercing cries of despair. They held each other tightly and talked in blubbering snatches and whimpering bursts. A fierce heat breathed from his convulsing body. Stained with tears, their faces were torn and wet. He was unconscious, drained and empty, desolate and full of nothing. Crushed, his tear-filled unwavering eyes were fixed, staring blindly through the chair opposite and through the wall behind at the long view ahead, totally eaten-up, aching and paralysed with unbearable grief. Everything had changed. With his defences down, in desperate quivering gasps he confessed to their plans. Words incubated for a long time about marriage and children were blurted out in fits and starts. But it was too late. The chance had gone, gone forever. Temporarily, sleep brought relief and rescued him from his living hell. He was like his father, he put off and delayed, like sand he let life slip through his fingers, aimlessly drifting along, thinking that it would last forever. Her own opinions she kept to herself. She let him talk. Inside he was numb, he had died with her. It was so final. Nothing could bring her back. He was never, ever going to see her again, or hold her in his arms or talk on the phone. Distressed and swamped in sadness he struggled with his immeasurable pain. The depth of his anguish was overwhelming. With his light extinguished the harsh reality emerged. Over the years she had known many people to die, young and old and of course she had been shocked and sad and heart sorry for their families, tears had welled-up, but she had never cried, never like her son had wept. Exhausted, their grip slowly released. Then suddenly from nowhere an unforgettable chilling scream ripped through the room, resonating in her ears, ricocheting against the walls and left to echo in the quiet of the next day. "And they burnt her." Composing himself, he got up and left the room to start the long sad journey of grieving.

AUTUMN

Her husband had no appetite for winter. There was no purpose. There was nothing to chew at, no garden to dig, no seeds to sow, nothing to nurture. It was a waiting game. There was much sighing and closing of doors. Before her husband felt restored again, deep gulping clouds would swallow the sky whole, all the leaves would fall and rush around madly, bright and crisp or to become slippery in the rain, brushed together and collected in bags by the road sweeper or left wet to wilt, banked up in corners in brown heaps for hedgehogs to find or children to discover on their way home from school, when they would scuff around excitedly in their Wellington boots. In the vacuum of an opening door, stray leaves would propel themselves over the step to land on the mat in the hall or become caught in a spider's web, suspended. Beads of dew irrigated the thirsty earth. Hoarfrost in the low light of morning would glisten on grass cut short in October and as the earth turned so it became half white and half green until it was all green. The orgy of Christmas and its furore had to be endured. Already he had said about getting this and that which surprised her for he didn't like the fuss and the constant reminder of it, but when it came to it, he liked it too, especially seeing the children. It was a time for them. He went shopping. She could tell by his smug expression and he was proud of the fact that he had bought her something she would love. Her days paid no attention to the seasons. They had their own timetable governed by 'use by' dates and the 'just in time' system. On a daily basis time fell into twelve-hour slots. Often she would find herself checking the time, either in the morning, standing in the kitchen, filling the kettle or in the evening preparing dinner, or if home early, eating dinner and the hands of the clock would be straight up and down, exactly six o'clock. As terms neared their end so the pace increased and time became even more valuable. Not being part of this feeling of his, it was hard for her to sympathise. It was up to him in a big way and her in a small way to make the next few months as good as possible. She tried her best to keep him motivated and cajoled and encouraged all the time to get out and about in spite of the weather. The poplars opposite, having outstayed their welcome, had been felled, the one remaining in the view from their window bent and leaned in the wind and it was the gauge with which to check the suitability for fishing. From their bed it was possible to see at a glance if it was worth getting up for. He took to the river, where they used to go a long time ago, and cast his line adrift. And then that time between January and March, when eventually summer time begins again, but nonetheless an inert time, still a time of hibernation, cold and raw, dull sunless days, admittedly getting longer all the time but still no reprieve from the knots of cold and biting winds, she continued to plan little interludes of activity so that he would write in his diary, Land Rover back, Smiths tribute band at the Stables, Guy went to Chicago, cricket in Brisbane, winning the cricket in Adelaide, cricket in Perth, retaining the Ashes in Melbourne, where they knew the ground, where even she was bowled over, remembering the city and catching the bus to St Kilda and swimming in the Southern Ocean, the actual road that the bus travelled was the road named on the address of a video she used in the classroom, and she imagined the ships a hundred years ago arriving from remote parts of the British Isles and roads and areas being named after them, keeping the 'new' immigrants in touch with 'home', winning the series in Sydney, sitting up all night to watch the matches, enduring the cold, his hands tucked under his arms, to watch the afternoon move across the wicket, Louise's book published, broad beans sown, went to see 'Forest' and they won, planning the next holiday. What more did he want?

As she kicked off her shoes on the mat in the hall she could see a letter lying casually on the dining room table. No ordinary letter. Picking it up, she turned it over. It had a soft delicate feel and The Ottoman Hotel was scrolled in pale gold lettering and its address, also in a band of gold edged the envelope. It had been posted in Istanbul and was heady with eastern promise. Reading the letter took her to an exotic city of jewelled minarets and mosques and hazy pink mornings and the heat and the intoxicating scents of spices and the pavements where you stepped aside men sitting on their haunches in doorways, and the wafting call to prayer, marking time, a sultry perfume of danger and excitement and magic carpets, sultans and tasselled slippers that curled up at the toes. The relaxed, easy scrawl written by her friend who had something important to say was enjoying a city break and while away, she had read her book. "Many thanks for your brilliantly written book *Patchwork*. I have just finished reading it and found that I couldn't really put down but one has to sleep and go sightseeing. I felt really moved by your writing, some of it quite magical and some very sad, such turmoil. It was a privilege to read your story and a book I shall always treasure."

It was a cold grey November day. Of course sun would have been better, but for once she didn't mind the drab colourless view from the train. Travelling early enough to get a window seat on the left she looked out over the familiar view. Cloud and mist hung and clung, mysteriously shrouding tracks of breathlessly still trees, their crowns thinning, waiting for the last growl of wind to hurtle their leaves to the ground. The still black slip of the canal, fringed neatly with a clipped brush of hedge, like that of a draught excluder on a revolving door, threaded its way silently between the brown ploughed fields. Beside it was a narrow ribbon of path, chalky white in places and trampled and trodden by dog walkers in others and once laboured by horses along the network of watery highways until the zip of rail abruptly ended the short working life of the canals. Further on, expensive thoroughbred horses stood patiently in groups, sending-up breathy clouds, waiting for their wealthy sporting owners to turn up and pamper and indulge. Sheep ambled slowly, nuzzling and gleaning from what was left of the dew soaked end-of-season grass. The view had gone. Turning back to the A-Z on her lap she tried to work out the best and most economical use of her time until one o'clock when she was meeting her children for lunch. The smooth uninterrupted journey transported her too early for the shops to be open. It had been her intention all week to get away, to fade into obscurity in the pavement crush or the choked underground or sit out of sight and gaze blankly at nothing in particular, anonymous, alone with her thoughts. She bought a coffee and sat quietly in the corner staring at the backs of customers queuing for their skinny lattes and tempting pastries, using cards or rummaging in purses and pockets for change. Her son's sudden tragic loss overshadowed everything. Her own troubles seemed irrelevant and paled into insignificance. Increasingly she felt remorse, ashamed that she had indulged in propagating a personal vendetta and a vindictive meaningless blight to sabotage her husband. The terrible, terrible episode brought them together again.

They all thought that the waitress who approached was going to talk, as they had been, about the paisley shirt she was wearing, resurrected from the eighties and worn by her son years ago for a school do, though seeing it again now, he could not believe that he had. Instead she launched into the wonder of her hair. They laughed. As always, with her children, she was herself. Nearby was a Dr Martin shop, nothing more than a few shoes and a few pallets and harsh yellow lighting warmed with electric stand-alone heaters that belted out enough heat to melt and must have cost a fortune. As soon as she set eyes on the shoes, they were hers. Taking her son in to approve was just a formality.

CHRISTMAS

The diet of programmes served over the holidays left her feeling undernourished and in spite of the freezing conditions she was glad to get outside. Embracing the cold, she and her son took the 'circular' walk. She had walked it many times but never in snow, good deep snow. Once off the glassy paths, where on the point of slipping over, arms flew out suddenly to right the inevitable fall, their feet pressed into the crisp white surface. Others too had walked, the imprints of their boots and shoes and trainers clearly visible, walking to and fro, the snow compacted at stiles and kissing gates. The walk took them across fields, around fields, along farm tracks and across the slippery distance of compressed snow between the farmhouse and the barns where the collie came to see them off. A flock of fat fleeced sheep, beige against the smothering of white, grazed, shuffling and snuffling for grass. It was while they were skirting the river, stopping now and then to capture the scene with clumsy gloved hands that they disturbed the barn owl. With food being scarce, he was hunting, looking for the faintest movement along the tangled riverbank in its desperate search for a vole or an unsuspecting warbler finding itself in the wrong place at the wrong time. Catching his haunting creamy-fawn plumage and broad deliberate wingspan in the pale half-light he soundlessly slipped from a branch in the willow and swooped low and silently along to the next tree. Her camera was ready. He was illusive. After several attempts they left him in his pursuit of meagre rations, trudging on towards the road then back across the field to the farm. Frozen in time, the shallow sun lit the desolate scene, the only sign of life being the occasional soot-black crow and the fresh tracks of a whiskery Mr Fox, who the night before, under a ringing steely sky had made his way down towards the farm buildings in search of something tasty to eat, like a chicken.

All around him the grass reappeared. Gradually the snowman at the end of the garden was reduced to the size of a milk bottle. The month-long siege ended and when it was green again her husband insisted that they went out in the car. Water instead of snow spilled across paths and the roads, mingling with the loose slush, dripping into drains. Cars travelled confidently along the road outside the house. Out and about the salted roads were black with dirt, gloopy puddles lay around, along with abandoned carpets, heaped at the side of the road, where cars the previous week had struggled to get a grip in the snow. Not discerning, the crows fell amongst the discarded remnants, pecking and picking and searching for morsels, oblivious to the stale choking smell emitted from the recycled packaging. Her husband had been back to the reservoir recently, on his own, to remember and remind himself of that time and had a great desire to take her to where he had learnt to swim in the hot summer of 1959, when he was ten. They had been before, a long time ago. But it was different now, or rather her husband was different now. Apart from the water level being lower, the reservoir was much the same. Ducks and coots gathered where it was free of ice, preening and pruning. As they walked round, passed the big lump of concrete on the clearly visible beach an image appeared in the distant horizon of his mind, of his father in his swimming trunks. There was a photograph. He told her and showed her where he had swam, using a strong front crawl, trying to instil confidence in his children. He had been forty-two. In the silence of winter, almost devoid of life and looking eerily dead, it was hard to imagine as the mist lifted and rolled, encircling the frozen water she could hear the air ringing with laughter and giggles as the family she had become part of splashed about in the blistering heat. That evening she limboed under the Christmas tree in search of the green tin box containing the old photographs.

She had spent, it seemed to her the entire fortnight keeping the food supplies at their optimum. The fridge groaned. A random selection of neatly labelled cake tins were comfortingly filled with mince pies and shortbread and Battenburg and caramel shortbread, ready to accompany the endless cups of teas and coffees. All morning her children slept and dozed, reluctant to leave the dopey warmth of their beds, each appeared at different times and in the kitchen there was a steady flow of activity, making breakfast, and elevenses and lunch and everything in between that called for seasonal treats, straddled from seven am until two. Then of course, for her, it was time to think about dinner. Ensuring that everyone was fed and watered, that clothes were washed and dried and folded and returned to the rightful owner, that the bathroom, which was under enormous pressure, especially as the outside toilet was frozen, was scum-free and that the toilet rolls were replenished daily was in itself a full time job. Due to the adverse weather her plans for the holidays had failed to materialize. Instead, she spent her time quietly clearing the kitchen from the midnight feasts the previous night, sorting the ever-accumulating rubbish, wiping and mopping the streaming condensation from the windows so that she could see outside. Occasionally she made a nest out of cushions and read her book or the paper or did a crossword from the book of crosswords or just dozed. Sometimes a fleeting glimpse of her son came into her mind and she wondered how he was coping with his loss. His brothers had kept him up-beat and buoyant and both he and the household fell quiet as they packed their things and left. It had been a good holiday. Wrapped and packed and tied with bows she had been showered with love, made to feel special and adored. Included. For her husband, reaching 1 January was a milestone. Without fail, the daylight hours would start to stretch out again. He tended not to get too involved with the festivities and found it easy to forget the hangover of Christmas, the clutter and indulgencies of the previous week, quietly slipping back into his routine, unlike her, he did not feel deflated, life continued as normal.

She didn't have the burning anticipation of a year ago. There had been too many distractions. Looking back, the space between the stars had been uneventful and clouded with sadness. Normality returned however, and the outlook seemed bleak. In Bargain Booze beer, wines and spirits were being re-priced, ready for the VAT increase. Likewise, garages sported queues of cars, their drivers anxious to fill their tanks, albeit until the following week, when by then the petrol would be used up and they would need more, the total saving amounting to hardly anything, a drop in the ocean.

Her pessimism was short lived. Already a number of things had occurred. Firstly, there on the publisher's website was her book, listed as 'coming soon'. Then, a week later everything about it was listed. Amazon too, had the details. Hovering excitement began to possess her and she found it hard to concentrate. With her spirits elevated, she forged ahead and wrote to 'Look East'; to be honest she expected nothing more than an acknowledgement, but her drive and enthusiasm didn't waver. Also she heard from a publication that she subscribed to, that she had emailed in the holidays about reviewing her latest book, saying that as soon as she had a copy, would she send it. Then, after its long convalescence the Land Rover was finally reunited with her husband, fit and healthy, its gleaming undercarriage was just longing to be christened with a good splattering of mud. Six months had passed since it had so miserably failed its MOT. Looking at the state of the corrosion, Dave thought it had been used to haul boats out of the sea and up onto the beach. Bought on eBay, it had originally been sourced from Sheffield on the strength of it being what she wanted, stressed and old and green and although it had a valid MOT at the time, it was clearly not going to get another without undergoing major invasive surgery. It was like Trigger's broom that had had a new handle and a new head but was the same broom, likewise, everything that could be replaced had been replaced but it was the same Land Rover. Then as she idly scrolled through the Eaton Bray website, she could see that a new entry had appeared. The person had been born in the same house that she had lived in as a child. Now she might be able to throw some light on the boy in the square photograph. Hastily she emailed and sent the photographs. It was astonishing to think that after years of searching that she might learn more about him. And the tights, mislaid for three weeks turned up. Already she had searched drawers and stood on a chair to reach into the airing cupboard in case they had somehow become folded in the sheets. It was unlikely. Her mind kept returning to when and where she last saw them and it maddened her that they were not clearly visible especially considering that one pair was the seasonal red. Her husband thought that she had thrown them out with the rubbish over Christmas. Why would she not notice? No, they were around somewhere. She failed to see how they could simply disappear. Her organisation in the wardrobe department was second to none. Nothing escaped her, at any one time she knew exactly what was in the wash basket, and what was in the drawer. She made a mental note of the whole week's outfits in advance, especially important as pupils who saw her on a weekly basis immediately recognised something worn the previous week. No detail was spared, hair bands, shoes, earrings, all chosen with care. "She had those on last week." They would say. She could hear them. Again she systematically removed each drawer and searched. Miraculously there they were, bundled together as she had placed them in the drawer, red, navy and brown. Somehow they had become suspended in the gap behind the drawers, the thin nylon fibres had hooked themselves to the roughly hewn surface of the wooden interior. Brushing off the drift of grey fluff that clung to them she was jubilant.

The local newspaper, often not received, was folded and pushed with some force through the letterbox, it fell, distributing its innards of glossy fliers and adverts to the floor behind the curtain. Gathering it all up, she laid it on the kitchen table, dividing and removing the sections, property, motors and the Go that she didn't look at and placed them ready for recycling by the back door. As she proceeded to make dinner she turned the pages of what was left, not reading anything in particular, but glancing at the headlines and looking more closely at the photographs. Some parts were totally uninteresting and rapidly turned the pages until the obituaries, towards the end, where she slowed right down casting her eyes slowly and systematically over the two pages, checking names and ages. She closed the paper, but not before noticing a name in the bottom right hand corner, a familiar name, she was the same age as her. Along with the others, she put it in the recycling bin. Until the next day her friend kept reappearing in her mind. Forty years had effortlessly slipped past. She remembered the immense fun that they had shared at college, at their work placement, shopping in Chelsea Girl, shopping in Biba and Mr Freedom, trying on hats in British Home Stores, following Alan Clark of the Hollies, she had the smallest feet and indulged in the most outrageous shoes and she thought about the picture, taken in Paris of the two of them, posing for the camera, smooth skinned faces, eyes bright, hair shinning, everything to aspire to and live for, their whole future ahead. Now it was all to look back on. Was it her friend? Feeling unsettled she retrieved the paper from the bin and called the funeral director dealing with the arrangements. It was her friend. And as if the sadness of her dying was not enough, the tragic circumstances of her death were even worse. A week later at the crematorium, she expected to see a host of family and friends, cars, coming from all over, swinging into parking spaces, dark suited men sporting various strengths of designer stubble, artists, there would have been artists, defying the rules, wearing denim and vivid colours, women veiled and gloved, clanking inappropriately in black patent stilettos, much hugging and holding, the sound of hushed words and muffled sobs, a quiet cigarette to steady the nerves, the quiet curl of smoke. Her career had been filled with high fashion, she had travelled, taken risks, been at the centre of decision making. Over the years, millions of pounds had been made out of her sought after creations and 'must haves'. The image of the fashion industry could not have been further from the truth. 'Like a candle in the wind', it summed-up what a shallow futile business it was. Including her, there were six mourners.

Sweet the rain's new fall sunlit from heaven,
Like the first dewfall on the first grass.
Praise for the sweetness of the wet garden,
Sprung in completeness where his feet pass.

THE ADRENALIN RUSH

All day she was levitated above the ground, a smile permanently pasted across her face. The day moved effortlessly. *Domestic Science* was published, exactly two years after her first book. Her exaggerated exhilaration was compounded further when she got home and opened the brown cardboard box. Inside, was her second book, twelve copies, flat and glossy, freshly sliced on the guillotine. Lifting one out, she opened it, the pen and ink drawings complemented each of the twelve chapters and in the front, the layout, the dedication and the acknowledgements were all as she had requested. Taking a copy she placed it on the bookshelf between *Patchwork* and *Nigella Express*. Running parallel with her excitement was an unexpected request to do an interview for The Food Programme on Radio 4 and although completely unrelated to her book, the initial contact had been because of it. It was to be the following Wednesday in her classroom. Suddenly, she had a streaming cold and when it got too much she went to the fridge and took out a fiery red chilli, cut it in half and smeared the glistening juices on her upper lip and around her nose. Instantly her skin flared an angry red as though she had shaved. It nipped like mad and reduced her to tears but the clear breathing was vital for the morning ahead. Killing two birds with one stone, an unfortunate phrase, she launched into letting everyone she knew either by letter or email or phone about the forthcoming interview and the recent publishing of her book. Originally the interview was to be held in a local radio station, but the producer phoned back, keen to have culinary sound effects in the background, could he come into school. Even before the register was taken, a brand new flask fell to the floor, shattering its thin silver glass. Out with the broom. And a pupil didn't like the state of the aprons, complaining bitterly about each one as she unhooked it from the peg. Immediately she scooped all twenty aprons in her arms, dumped them in the storeroom and collected a clean armful from behind the door. Of course these mishaps did not appear on the programme, instead it started by her talking about preparing vegetables for minestrone soup, small enough to fit on a spoon. Others too contributed but the programme returned to her classroom where the airwaves were hers and she talked about the importance of retaining food within the curriculum and where the pupils were keen to give their enthusiastic opinions about 'Cooking in Schools.'

Not ten miles away was the mighty Amazonian warehouse, ruinous to small independent bookshops and a rival to others. And no wonder, it was cheaper, no petrol, no car parking charges and easier, just sit at home while watching television and at the click of the mouse your book would be delivered within forty eight hours. Aptly named, its Leviathan size was breathtaking and probably visible from outer space, certainly from the motorway. It was set in a swathe of derelict wasteland littered with the debris, remnants of the once flourishing brickworks, needed a long time ago to address the shortfall in housing stock to replace the crumbling Victorian terraces. No attention had been spared on its basic box structure. Within the faceless walls, she imagined fleets of forklift trucks, conveyor belts and computer screens, marshalling books and all manner of goods 'from every department' imported in huge container lorries from China, the cheap sweaty pungent chaos emptied and checked only to be packed and redistributed again with only a handful of staff overseeing the operation.

On Sunday she went to London and combined a viewing of her son's work in a North London Gallery with the ten o'clock service at St Martin in the Fields. Although the pre-Christmas snow had curtailed her, her desire to go to the service was as strong as ever. As she surfaced from the underground the ringing peal greeted her. The few tourists, already in Trafalgar Square were paying no attention to the small unpretentious church in the far corner. She had known about the church for a long time and admired the tireless work that they did for the less fortunate. How lovely it seemed to walk in off the street. Taking a pew, she compared it with others, the church was surprisingly plain and for that she liked it all the more, the service too was not grand. The chancel window was a joy. To her the plain-lattice leaded window symbolised that that there was always a way through adversity. She felt comfortable and welcomed. The sermon was about turning the other cheek. It was a tall order. Temptation and diversion was greater than ever, people were swallowed up with commercialism and consumerism. Leaving the church she crossed the road and headed for The National Gallery to take in the Impressionists. After the comfort of Christianity it was cold and comfortless in the real world. No one offered help to the mum trying to bump her twin buggy up two flights of steps and so without thinking and as though it was nothing, she took hold of the end of it. The mum thanked her over and over. To be able to stand and savour such works of art so closely, to actually see the brush strokes, to observe the scene, to be there was special. And the time that it took, not the one second press of a button, but hours, days, weeks, months, years, maybe. Navigating her way to meet her son at Angel tube at two, she dropped in to the main bookshops en route to make some hopefully useful contacts and into the British Museum to check out the African Rooms, the workmanship in carved door and the roundness of the terra cotta pots, the chair made of weapons. It was raw and bitterly cold waiting for her son and she wrapped her hands round the paperboard cup of coffee for warmth. Together they went off to the gallery, he knew the way and she obediently followed, glad of his company. The show was called The Colour of London and had come about to demonstrate that London had a lot to offer and was not all doom and gloom. Her son's picture showed a row of industrial units painted in livid stripes behind which was a rusting bulging gasometer set against a stunning blue sky. Afterwards, they went for some food in Byrons, a totally different concept to their usual eateries. The raw under-construction interior left nothing to be desired. They sat at a table for two overlooking a side street on old school chairs. Hers was a worn out yellow. Nothing matched. Pipe work, extraction and electrics were all clearly visible. It was more like a fashionable up-market transport café with sauce bottles to match, introduced she was sure as part of the raft of austerity measures besieging the country, to accommodate the downturn in peoples eating habits. While she indulged in macaroni cheese with courgette chips and knickerbocker glory her son went for a burger and fries, followed by a wedge of chocolate brownie to settle his delicate state. As always she kept parting brisk and business like and on reaching Angel again they hugged and said goodbye. On the train home she dozed between stops.

Like a terrier with a bone she was hungry for leads and information and gnawed away at her research, coming back over and over again, reassessing the evidence. She checked QDBM suggested by Brian, who at the time of sending the message was evacuating his house for higher ground, as flooding in Queensland was imminent. It did not provide anything useful. Other names were coming into view. A local village website was proving useful and she contacted Colleen who had lived in her house after her and Mary who had lived next door and Roger in the US had lived at number 49 in 1958. Again she wrote to Mary and enclosed a stamped addressed envelope hoping to tug at her memories even though in her heart she felt that she wasn't interested and couldn't be bothered. Would she discard the envelope, or shred it or stuff it in a drawer? And what if she threw it away then decided later that she did have something to say. Trying to get a different slant on things she posted fresh messages on Genes Reunited. Replies felt that it would be impossible to search for someone without a name. It was a lost cause. She looked at placing an advert in the announcements section of various papers, but the cost seemed prohibitive.

The next Women's Institute meeting was Monday 4 July in the Village Hall. She would go. Driving the twenty miles was no trouble. Frequently she opened the windows to rid the car of the warm humid air. Rows of chairs had been arranged in the small carpeted room for approximately twenty women and cups and saucers laid for the all-important cup of tea, served by the ladies on duty, when the visiting speaker had finished. The ladies were welcoming and curious when she sat amongst them, wanting to know who she was and why she was there. She said that she hoped to be able to speak to someone who remembered the village sixty years ago and was advised to speak to Gladys who had lived in the village all her life. After the formalities and the interesting talk from Sandra the magistrate, she made a bee-line for the octogenarian sitting on the front row. Finding that they had lots in common she showed her the small square photograph. Gladys felt sure that she remembered her surname but was unable to recognize the boy. Gladys had a daughter, Sarah, who surprisingly lived nearby. Five times she called, at work, on holiday, shopping, out. At last she was in. From her bag she carefully took out the envelope containing the photos. Alas Sarah didn't recognize the boy in the square photo but she did provide her with some new names to follow up. Eagerly she jotted them down.

On Saturday she went to check them out. Straight away she had to leave the first name on the list as her address was merely the name of the road, the second person was out as, too was the fourth, the third name however, proved to be useful in that he suggested a further name to check in the next village, in a narrow lane that once led to meadowsows but had become filled in with desirable houses. He was happy to stand and talk on the step and she was happy to listen with the sun on her back. Leaving him to contemplate the memories stirring in his mind she went off to find Bruce. She parked the car and went over to the man who had just called on a neighbour. The face seemed not unfamiliar. "I'm looking for Bruce Westman." She said. "I am Bruce." Like Tim on the tractor, it was his father's face that she remembered. She told him who she was and where she had lived and who her father was. Instantly he remembered a rare and intimate sight, of himself as a child, standing at the end of the terraced row peering down the communal path that ran between the houses and the outside toilets and seeing a vision of her mother drying and brushing the tangles of her long auburn coloured hair out in the shambles of a garden. Had she been aware of anyone seeing her or paying attention to her, she would have been mortified and what an unusual sight for a small boy to witness and remember for fifty-five years. "It came right down her back."

He continued. And he showed her on his own, how far down. She said that she had never ever seen her mother's hair loose. Remembering how small the scullery was and that she would have had no means of washing and drying hair as long as it had been described, doing it outside might have been the best option. "You're like your mother." He said. They stood shirt sleeved and bare armed in 'the warmer than average for the time of year' October sunshine and she declined when he asked if she would like to come in. She could see that he had left his door was ajar while popping to his neighbour across the road but she was happy to stand in the glorious golden warmth. She showed him the photo and described the photo of Mary and her playing at the back door. His mind was scanning his own archive of pictures, wanting her to see them. She would be impressed. And so for a moment or two while he fired up his computer she found herself in the smallest space, really used for hanging coats but converted to a mini office, on the other side of the front door, thankfully still not closed. While the computer was coming to life he produced a great bundle of old photos. There was Mary with her 'big' hair along with a lot of other people, who, if they were alive could maybe give her some answers. Bruce was enthusiastic and recommended further names that could be useful. Back outside in the bright sun-washed road they said goodbye and would be in touch if other things sprung to mind. Peter lived in a close that had been named after the headmistress of the village school and his enthusiasm for family history matched Bruce's. In those few minutes on the doorstep they shared a desire, a passion to find out more about the past and how it was. Once he sunk his teeth into the information it was extraordinary that within a few moments how very nearly everyone in Victoria Terrace, although he didn't call it that, he called it Middle Row, was named. Chewing over the words, absorbed he absentmindedly took the palm of his hand around his chin. She left a message at the local electrical/bike shop and the next evening Janet phoned, keen as mustard to share her story.

Having exhausted all avenues, she finally got in touch with

the Falkirk Herald with the view of placing an advert, and the Watford Observer and Leamington Courier hoping that her story might be of interest to the local community and capture the attention of an elderly resident without feeling embarrassed. And so the drama unfolded. The advert idea was soon abandoned as it was hugely expensive and so instead she wrote, asking if her pictures along with a hint of her story could be told. Kirsty requested a telephone interview and it was duly arranged for Monday morning and emailed for her to check. Over the weekend Andrene got in touch. She was a second cousin once removed, whatever that meant. She had been researching family history and tracing relatives back as far as 1700 and was positive that her father was her father's uncle and had his birth certificate. Replying to her email she said that she would need to redesign the family tree with twigs and offshoots. It transpired that there were a further three aunts born after the siblings named on her father's army record. She wanted Andrene to ask her father what he could remember of his uncle. After her early excitement however, her enthusiasm dwindled. He had nothing to say.

By seven on Friday morning on her way to the bank she stopped off to buy a Watford Observer. Folding it in half she walked as calmly as possible the length of the newsagents and back out into the crisp October air to the car parked in the lay-by. Once settled and the door closed she opened the paper, rapidly turning the hot-off-the-press newsprint until page thirty four. On the 'Nostalgia' page were her two photographs. They looked good, clear and not as grainy as she thought they might. Now would anyone recognize the children and would they get in touch? And was this going to end her five year search?

Returning to the villages on the Bedfordshire/ Buckinghamshire border she called again on the people who had been out to find that they were still out. It was Wednesday and they had been collected on the mini-bus and taken for lunch. They were real gadabouts. Again she called on Iris. It had been three years since she had seen Iris. But Iris's memory was good, remembering her and her story. In that time she had thought but could add no more.

Janet, who had phoned, suggested the local magazine and went off to locate one on the overcrowded desk. It was delivered to every resident, read and reread, referred to for a plumber or gardening services or aerial problems and kept handy until the next issue was slipped through the letterbox. It was a way of uniting and bringing together some sort of community spirit or link that, like other things over the years, had become lost. People liked reading about their local news, they liked seeing photographs and their names in print. In her house she too had a similar magazine. It sat on the side and she dipped into it while waiting for the potatoes to boil or having breakfast. The next day she wrote a piece and sent the photos. Within moments the reply came back saying that it would be in the next issue. Wow. She got wind that it was in circulation and it wasn't long before she received an email from the editor. Would she call this number. The woman she phoned knew her, she had lived in the same road, gone to the same school. They shared teacher's names, long forgotten.

Margaret didn't mind admitting that Victoria Terrace or Middle Row was where the worthless scum of the earth lived, the dregs of society, the flotsam, washed-up on the outskirts of the village, living in a squalid terrace of crumbling brickwork, peeling paint and limited sanitation. 'Nice' people implied that they didn't really know the lane or its inhabitants. They were being polite. They didn't want to know.

Before meeting her father, her mother had enjoyed a social life that left her dancing, singing and laughing long into the night. She ate lobster and wore beautiful dresses in lovely fabrics, cut on the bias, grosgrain, a flash of red velvet, spangled. She was accustomed to polished oak floors thrown with Persian rugs, wood panelled rooms lined with books, high ceilings, china, crystal, silver and linen. Meeting him however reduced her life to a silent scream. It became a life of nothing more than drudgery and impoverished squalor, a penny pinching existence, nails bitten to the quick, ruled with a rod of iron and finding herself in such a shabby hovel after the gusto of fine living sickened her. She was desperate to leave the misery behind but there was no going back. Battered, bruised and broken she 'took the bull by the horns' spending her entire life clawing her way back to respectability and the elegance that she once enjoyed.

Margaret said that she knew a couple of elderly ladies who would remember. Enid and Hilda confirmed Iris's account of nothing short of a tabloid scandal, fuelling gossip that had lasted sixty years; that her father was living with a woman half his age when her mother swept in carrying their baby wrapped in a hand knitted shawl. A terrible scene broke out. Like spiteful cats they hissed and scratched and clawed until her mother was triumphant. Ousted, the lover quickly made a hasty exit to a house four doors away. So was the boy in the square photo their son? Enid and Hilda could remember no more, or did they too close ranks, some prying outsider was too close for comfort. Now knowing the name of the woman and the names of her children, she checked their dates of birth and where they were registered, she left a message on Genes Reunited. There was a cautious reply wanting to know if she had genuine reasons for wanting to find out the names before divulging details. Eventually she convinced her of wanting nothing more than to check the children in the photographs and she emailed the address. Without hesitation she found the street map, checked the locality and went the next day. Not even the sun-visor provided enough shade on that startlingly bright winter afternoon. Where the absence of sun had prevented a thaw, hard white shapes were stamped against hedges and buildings. She parked in front of a beige coloured Audi, its windscreen, even at one thirty, still encrusted in rime. Sitting for a few moments in the shadow of number 71, she prepared her introduction and unnecessarily checked the address again. It was a nice house and the shrubs and grasses in the front garden had been carefully chosen and lovingly looked after. As she rang the bell she could see through the frosted glass door. The post lay on the mat. There was no one in. Disappointed, she rang the bell again, then reluctantly turned and went back to the car.

Curious to know one way or the other, she returned a week later. Ringing the bell brought a low woof and through the frosted glass this time she could see the blurry mirage of an ageing collie. He would have sensed her, a stranger as she parked the car and walked the few yards to the front door. Unlike the previous week, she could hear a movement and the door opened.

"Are you Mrs Reddings?" She enquired.

"Yes."

"And is your husband's name Michael J Reddings?"

"Yes."

"Well … " And in the briefest of moments she outlined why she was standing on the step. Mrs Reddings invited her in and fetched her husband from the garage. There was much to explain and exchange. Photograph albums were pored over and she placed her two small black and white pictures on the table, they scrutinized the small pale faces, cross-referencing the parting in the hair, its curliness, the depth of the forehead and the skin tone. There was undoubtedly a likeness or did they want there to be? Auntie Molly would know. Mike and Sandra took her shopping on Fridays and would ask her. Would Auntie Molly spill the beans and surrender her secrets, finally fitting the lost parts of the puzzle or like others would she too remain loyal to the end?

The war seemed to bring out the worst in people, the confused uncertainty provided an excuse to throw caution to the wind and indulge unrestricted and immune to law and order and moral codes. Nothing mattered. Live for the moment. It was easy to operate below the radar, escaping detection, or to move about and get lost in the endless tide of disruption. Too much was going on for authority to worry about petty discrepancies. Maybe even more so in rural communities, where away from the constant fear of bombing familiar in the larger towns and cities, there was a cherished camaraderie. Everyone was in the same boat and apart from the transient population, the eager fresh faced youths, who in their innocence could not comprehend the horrors of war, going off to do their 'bit', the ghosts of faceless men returning from what they had seen and migrants, lost, going nowhere, life went on almost unchallenged. Her father had been one of those, lawless, unaffected, living the good life, getting away with murder, a woman here a woman there, their defences off guard, flattered by his smooth talking, sucked in by his sly smiling eyes.

Michael had never questioned that his father was not named on his birth certificate or that he had his mother's surname. At times he seemed frustratingly vague. It was rumoured that his father was from a POW camp nearby. He remembered the man who lived with his mother and remembered going with them to the school near Kings Langley where her exemplary father, according to his reference had been or was the engineer/handyman and her mother the cook/housekeeper. She could see him recalling the lasting memory of the tree lined drive and the grace and beauty of the school set amongst the trees. She asked him if he could remember her mother arriving with a baby and him leaving to move along the road with his mother. He said that really he had not paid much attention and was not aware and that due to overcrowding in the house he was often not living with his mother but with his grandmother or auntie. She had so wanted him to tell her how it had been, hoping that he would remember as she had done.

Eagerly she waited, impatient for Friday. Auntie Molly said that she almost certain that Michael's mother and her father had not had children. There was a to-do but she refused to be drawn into saying anything she might regret. The good thing for Michael was that she gave him his father's name. Auntie Molly's information was not enough. Feeling sure that she knew more, she sent the two photographs for Sandra and Michael to show her on their next visit. There was a reply. Aunty Molly didn't want to be troubled with photographs and it was all so long ago. "She doesn't want to speak about it although she said that Jock was a bully and wore a masonic ring, She said that he was charming when they first met but later would not allow Gwen to visit her family down the road, and they were not allowed up there. He also made her scrub the floors every morning before work". She pestered Michael about his sister Shirley. "Shirley lives in Great Yarmouth. I phoned her and she doesn't remember anything as she wasn't born until 1953. She says that Gwen once told her that she lived with Mrs Weir (her mother) as they were overcrowded in their house."

Little bursts of information lubricated and kept her interest. Via the village website she contacted Roger again. His aunt's name had come into conversation and she found that she lived in a nearby village, safely installed behind high wrought iron gates only accessible by speaking into the electronic code lock. Roger suggested calling his uncle and as soon as she had cleared the table, she did. Gordon remembered her father and the awful commotion when her mother arrived. He remembered her 'red' hair worn up in a bun.

"And what was it your mother made?"

"Shortbread." Renowned for her shortbread prowess, it was the obvious answer.

"No, it wasn't shortbread … It rotted your teeth."

"Fudge," she said.

"That was it. Fudge."

Having exhausted all avenues, she would call it a day and resign herself to never completely knowing who the boy in the square photograph was and although her indulgent desire to know would always be there at the back of her mind she had to respect everyone's loyalty and their personal reasons for not talking. At the time they had given their word, they had promised not to tell. And did it matter?

THE PLASTIC FUNNEL

The need to buy a good sized funnel, because her husband was changing the oil in her car and needed to decant it into another container, took her to the 'pound' shop in town. On her way to the far end of the shop she was easily distracted by the array of cheap goods, stacked high on shelves and unreachable racking. Occupying a big square of space near the middle, the shrink wrapped, bulk buy toilet rolls stood their ground and next to them was the vast range of plastic storage containers cluttering the narrow aisles. Cleaning products lined the walls, multi-packs of dusters and cloths and all manner of household requisites including white enamel plates edged in blue, individually wrapped in tissue, like the dish that she used for rice pudding and 50 g balls of glistening nylon and car accessories and gardening necessities and DIY products, which through bitter experience she had found to be sub-standard and less than adequate. Finding the perfect funnel only took a moment and true to its claim, it cost a pound. Wondering back to the till she found herself caught up with what she assumed to be Radio 2 playing in the big airy vault above her. Calls and advice were pouring in to be aired. She lingered and listened, randomly looking at things that she had no intention of buying. On air people were sharing their feelings about partners, husbands and wives or colleagues who bullied, who hurt or intimidated or persecuted the weaker person by deliberately ignoring them. Many were aghast and some could not imagine the torment and uncertainty that ensued. Most callers recommended communicating or leaving. For her, that was easier said than done. From others, she learned to resist, to hang fire, to hold her tongue and bite the bullet. It was easier that way, leaving her situation to smoulder on the back burner.

That's just the way it is
Some things will never change
That's just the way it is,
that's just the way it is, it is, it is, it is

She was intuitive. She cleaned the entire fridge in her quest
to find the stump of ginger, even checking the compost in case
her husband had seen it before reaching the fridge and
assumed it to be finished with. It was there, she knew that it
would be, tucked inside the red pepper, behind the eggs. She
always knew if she had or hadn't got all the ingredients for
something, she knew if there was a napkin or a pillowslip
missing, or if she needed bleach, or had used the last of the
turmeric. Somehow she knew and she also sensed immediately
if there was something amiss or different or wrong. She had
only been gone an hour and in that time the atmosphere had
thickened. He was anxious and unsettled. His mouth was set
and his lack-lustre voice hummed bland tuneless notes through
gritted teeth. It was over nothing and nothing to do with her
but everything to do with a letter that required a phone call to
clear up a possible misunderstanding. He was not civil until he
had got it sorted.

"I knew." She said as she stood stirring the tea. "That
something had changed. Why is it me who has to bear the
brunt?"

"I didn't mean you any harm."

It didn't answer her question.

The more she thought about the situation she decided that
how she felt was her own fault. She needed to talk to get things
straight in her mind. For over two years she had tried to speak,
rearranging the words waiting in her head, waiting to be said.
And how she wanted to say them.

On Sunday evening she came close to talking. He was
standing on the landing, his hand on the newel cap about to go
downstairs. "I haven't found anything to watch." He
announced. She swivelled round, away from the computer
screen to face him. "We could have a conversation."

"What about?" He said.

"Well anything really. I like to talk."

"But you were in the sitting room and you didn't say anything."

"No. Because you don't want to talk." She wanted to add, "about those things under the stones", but she didn't. The noise of the television tightened the silence further. There was no need to talk. The people on the screen, as big as her, intruding in the corner of the sitting room had plenty to say. No, there was no need to talk and he avoided talking at all costs, preferring instead to talk about the weather, which unless she needed to get a line of washing dry was neither here nor there.

The moment had gone, again.

Another time she got a bit further. It came about by chance when they fell upon the subject of her approaching retirement. And although she felt too young to retire, it wasn't time to live on cups of pale weak tea and digestive biscuits, she wanted to finish work and do other things. Her husband said that they should talk as he didn't want her to think that it was necessarily a rosy picture. Of that she was well aware. "I too want to talk. I want to talk about the things under the stones. We'll talk tomorrow on the train." He seemed baffled. What did she mean, those things under the stones? They didn't talk about retirement or the things under the stones. It was too public an arena to be private. She had mixed feelings about retirement. In fact she was not keen on the word and when she had to give it as her reason for leaving, it seemed that the knell had rung. It conjured-up an image that she didn't think was for her. To start with she did not want to feel categorized or pigeon-holed. It was like being called a spinster or a pensioner. She worried silently about the looming fact of not going to work again and she didn't think that she would fare well as she spent most of her day with one eye on the clock. From the moment that she sprung out of bed and put her bare feet in her slippers she was fully occupied and was guilty of filling the day and guilty of not, cramming too much in, running out of time until the day came to an end and she would be disappointed at not completing what she set out to do. Very slightly over the years she demanded less of herself and instead of looking at what she had not done, she looked at what she had achieved over an hour or a day or a week. Observing her husband, she thought that he wasted a huge amount of time. Some days he had no plans, aimlessly drifting, not making good use of the day, sometimes surfacing mid-morning, breakfast, slipping towards eleven, time disappearing. Maybe that was how he saw retirement, not being governed by the hands of the clock. But it infuriated, she was like a pot coming to the boil, yet refusing to do so. And despite her tense hissing pressure she would simmer until something distracted her and the seething subsided and heat redistributed. She didn't think she could take-up daytime TV or mindless activities or launch into housework on a daily basis. She didn't want the highlight of the day to be changing the bed or putting the bins out, when for forty years they had not been worth mentioning. After the clutter of children and accumulation of possessions she had a great desire to transform the house to its former look, subtle hints, airy spaces, flowery wallpaper and chintz. She would have all the ingredients, energy and time and determination. Stripping wallpaper was a therapy in itself. Echoing rooms, carpets lifted, skirting stripped back to its knotty beginnings, sloughing off the years, removing the thin fragile layers, starting again.

Between Chicago and Denver she nearly spoke. They sat quietly immersed, mesmerised by the perpetual view. Connecting people were the scrawled wires written into the high plains, punctuated with telegraph poles. The scenery changed. The vegetation gave way to grassland, mile after mile after mile of faded yellowing scrub. Black glossy coated cattle grazed on the scented grass in the beating sun with only the occasional tree for shade. It was on the very tip of her tongue. In the distance, the big sky merged with the big land in a hazy blur.

While she wanted more than anything, to remove the noise from the picture she decided in the end to be philosophical and view her own situation as a failing of human nature; for her husband, he had some sort of barrier blocking out any reasonable way of addressing a situation or seeing another point of view and for her she was over sensitive to his stony silences, that in nearly fifty years she had failed to master. The programme reminded her that many others also endured this emotional backlash every now and then. And although her impetuous desire was to speak-up she was reticent and eventually resigned herself to saying nothing, to closing the drawer and slip quietly back into the comfortable routine that they usually shared, knowing in her heart and that in time he would erupt again, as he had that morning, and hoping that by then she would have the courage to confront the real problem lying beneath the surface. In the meantime she would chip away at her own failings. Brooding would change nothing. She thirsted for reconciliation with herself, to forgive and accept that she had whipped up such libellous accusations when most of the time he was how she wanted him to be. It had never been her intention to hurt or humiliate and felt ashamed. When she thought it was safe to do so, she finally relinquished the feeling of fear and dread that had beset her for two years. Instantly recognizable, the distinctive mix of the harpsichord and French horns playing the introduction of 'God Only Knows' by the Beach Boys came on the radio. Faint smiles melted their faces. It was their song.

I may not always love you
But as long as there are stars above you
You never need to doubt it
I'll make you so sure about it
God only knows what I'd be without you

If you should ever leave me
Though life would still go on believe me
The world would show nothing to me
So what good would living do me
God only knows what I'd be without you

Putting the knife down, she turned away from slicing the doughy bread and took his hardworking hands in hers and drew him towards her. "Remember," she said, "We've still got to have that chat."

General Bikram Singh wrote "A car is driven by looking through the windscreen and not through the rear view mirror. Whatever has happened should be left behind."

Acknowledgments

'Ten Story Love Song' Stone Roses
'God Only Knows' The Beach Boys
'Black Wings' Tom Waites
'That's just the way it is' Bruce Hornsby
'Morning has Broken' Eleanor Farjeon
'I vow to thee my country' Cecil Spring-Rice
'*Alice in Wonderland*' Lewis Carroll
'All Things Bright and Beautiful' Cecil F. Alexander
'*The Book of Common Prayer* (1662)'
Poem For Haiti Gillian Clarke
Thank you to NASA for the use of the image 'Deep inside the Milky Way'